Dead Giveaway

She started off, and Carter stopped her with his voice. "Where are we going?"

For the first time, the beauty-pageant smile disappeared and her lips became a tight line across her face. "I have my orders. I only do as I am told."

Her hesitation was enough. Carter started forward, but stopped when her hands came out of the pockets. Held steady, its barrel not wavering from Carter's chest, was a Rommer exactly like the one under his belt in the center of his back. . . .

FROM THE NICK CARTER
KILLMASTER SERIES

AFGHAN INTERCEPT
THE ALGARVE AFFAIR
THE ANDROPOV FILE
ARMS OF VENGEANCE
THE ASSASSIN CONVENTION
ASSIGNMENT: RIO
THE BERLIN TARGET
BLACK SEA BLOODBATH
BLOOD OF THE FALCON
BLOOD OF THE SCIMITAR
BLOOD RAID
BLOODTRAIL TO MECCA
BLOOD ULTIMATUM
THE BLUE ICE AFFAIR
BOLIVIAN HEAT
THE BUDAPEST RUN
CARIBBEAN COUP
CIRCLE OF SCORPIONS
CODE NAME COBRA
COUNTDOWN TO ARMAGEDDON
CROSSFIRE RED
THE CYCLOPS CONSPIRACY
DAY OF THE ASSASSIN
DAY OF THE MAHDI
THE DEADLY DIVA
THE DEATH DEALER
DEATH HAND PLAY
DEATH ISLAND
DEATH ORBIT
DEATH SQUAD
THE DEATH STAR AFFAIR
DEATHSTRIKE
DEEP SEA DEATH
DRAGONFIRE
THE DUBROVNIK MASSACRE
EAST OF HELL
THE EXECUTION EXCHANGE
THE GOLDEN BULL
HELL-BOUND EXPRESS
HOLIDAY IN HELL
HOLY WAR
HONG KONG HIT
INVITATON TO DEATH
ISLE OF BLOOD
KILLING GAMES
THE KILLING GROUND
THE KOREAN KILL
THE KREMLIN KILL

THE LAST SAMURAI
LAW OF THE LION
LETHAL PREY
THE MACAO MASSACRE
THE MASTER ASSASSIN
THE MAYAN CONNECTION
MERCENARY MOUNTAIN
MIDDLE EAST MASSACRE
NIGHT OF THE CONDOR
NIGHT OF THE WARHEADS
THE NORMANDY CODE
NORWEGIAN TYPHOON
OPERATION PETROGRAD
OPERATION SHARKBITE
THE PARISIAN AFFAIR
THE POSEIDON TARGET
PRESSURE POINT
PURSUIT OF THE EAGLE
THE RANGOON MAN
THE REDOLMO AFFAIR
REICH FOUR
RETREAT FOR DEATH
RUBY RED DEATH
THE SAMURAI KILL
SANCTION TO SLAUGHTER
SAN JUAN INFERNO
THE SATAN TRAP
SIGN OF THE COBRA
SINGAPORE SLING
SLAUGHTER DAY
SOLAR MENACE
SPY KILLER
THE STRONTIUM CODE
THE SUICIDE SEAT
TARGET RED STAR
THE TARLOV CIPHER
TERMS OF VENGEANCE
THE TERROR CODE
TERROR TIMES TWO
TIME CLOCK OF DEATH
TRIPLE CROSS
TUNNEL FOR TRAITORS
TURKISH BLOODBATH
THE VENGEANCE GAME
WAR FROM THE CLOUDS
WHITE DEATH
THE YUKON TARGET
ZERO-HOUR STRIKE FORCE

RUBY RED DEATH

KILL MASTER

NICK CARTER

JOVE BOOKS, NEW YORK

KILLMASTER #259: RUBY RED DEATH

A Jove Book/published by arrangement with
The Condé Nast Publications, Inc.

PRINTING HISTORY
Jove edition/March 1990

ISBN: 0-515-10274-1

Dedicated to the men and women of the
Secret Services of the
United States of America

ONE

August, 1944

The German SS office for the control of internal affairs in Romania was located in Bucharest, at 9 Straulesti Street. It was a three-story, gray stone building. Inside, the floors were chopped up into little cubicles designed to hold mostly file cabinets and few people.

Every hour on the hour for the last three days, Greta Schell left her cubicle and walked briskly down a long corridor to the office of the area commander, SS Gruppenführer Graf von Wassner.

It was four o'clock on the afternoon of August the twelfth. Greta ripped the last coded report from the machine and moved quickly. Her heels tapped heavily on the wooden floors bleached with too much scrubbing.

She knocked once on the glass pane of the door and

entered without a command. Wordlessly, she placed the report on the desk and stepped back to gauge its effect.

Von Wassner scanned the latest news quickly, and then read it a second time.

Dressed in the stark black uniform with the twin bolts of lightning on his collar, von Wassner was a striking figure. He stood to pace the room.

He was even more splendid to watch in motion than in repose. His thick blond hair and gray eyes glistened under the harsh lights as he walked with the lithe assurance of an acrobat. At forty-three he looked no more than thirty-five, and carried himself as if he felt another ten years younger than that.

Watching him, Greta Schell felt the same desire she had felt the first time she had slept with him a year before.

His voice, when he spoke, was a rumbling bass. "Hitler is an idiot and Himmler is his ass-kisser!"

"It is bad?"

He looked up. "Worse than bad. It is terrible. The partisans have linked up with the Red Army. They are in the Transylvanian Alps and pushing south."

The woman's lips quivered. "How long?"

"Two days, three at the most. Our mighty Führer has ordered us to hold Bucharest to the last man."

"Can we still get across the Danube to the sea?" Greta whispered.

Von Wassner nodded. "I think so. Order Dieter to bring the car around."

Greta Schell hurried from the office. Despite the horror of the moment, she had a slight smile on her lips.

He had not mentioned his wife in Berlin. She, Greta

Schell, had replaced her. Together, she and the count would be safe in South America.

Graf von Wassner stepped from the black Mercedes and leaned back through the window. "Take Fräulein Schell to her flat and return for me in an hour."

"Ja, Herr Gruppenführer."

The count hurried up the three flights, unlocked the door to his flat, and shoved it open.

One step into the room, von Wassner froze. Sitting in a chair, his hands folded across his fat paunch, was the head of the Bucharest Abwehr, Hermann Eisling.

Could the man know?

Von Wassner ignored the knot in his gut, shut the door, and stepped forward. He managed a look of contempt as he lit a cigarette.

"What the hell are you doing in my flat, Herr Eisling?"

"Waiting for you, of course."

"You have a key?"

"Locks are conceived by fools," the other man said with a shrug.

Von Wassner stepped to a nearby table and angrily extinguished the cigarette. "I've had a difficult day. What do you want?"

"Each day, in these times, is a difficult day."

"Dammit, Eisling—"

"I know," the Abwehr man interrupted.

"What?"

"I know of your plans. I know that you have purchased Portuguese passports for yourself and Fräulein Schell. I know that you have stolen a great amount of American dollars and English pounds sterling . . ."

Von Wassner bristled. "Eisling, do you know what you're saying?"

"Every word of it. I know that you plan to drive across the Danube to the Black Sea at Constanţa. There, you will—"

He was wearing a pair of blue trousers and a large turtleneck sweater, both of which showed his flab to disadvantage. Von Wassner took a firm hold on the bulk of the sweater, just under his chin, and yanked him up to a convenient position. He backhanded him across the mouth with his right hand. Then he let him have one from the opposite direction. He repeated the action half a dozen times. It was like hitting a punching bag. Eisling's head moved with the blows but he didn't resist, just hung loosely where he was held.

He whimpered once, and von Wassner let go of him. He flopped back down into the chair.

"What do you want?" von Wassner hissed.

Eisling didn't answer. Instead he took a handkerchief from one of his side trouser pockets and began dabbing at the blood that flowed from his nose and mouth and at the tears rolling down his cheeks.

"That wasn't necessary, Gruppenführer."

Von Wassner's foot shot forward. His toe connected squarely with Eisling's knee. The fat man squealed in pain and rolled from the chair to the floor.

"When I ask you a question, you answer me. Don't fuck around with it. Just answer."

"I want to come with you," Eisling whined.

Von Wassner yanked him to his feet. "You are a fool."

"Herr Gruppenführer, you might as well know that I

am an intelligent man and I accept the fact that I am a physical coward, so I won't fight you."

Von Wassner threw him back into the chair in disgust. From the holster at his belt he withdrew a 9mm Luger, cocked it, and placed the muzzle against the Abwehr man's head.

"I have to kill you."

"No, no, wait!" Eisling's lower lip quivered and more tears appeared on his cheeks. "The funds you have secured for your escape are not large. They are merely a fraction of what I can offer if you take me with you."

Von Wassner's grip relaxed slightly on the pistol. "What are you talking about?"

Eisling squirmed around in the chair, pulling himself together. He balled up the handkerchief and held it tightly in a fist as the arrogance began drifting back into his expression.

"I know where there are enough jewels to last both of us a lifetime, ten lifetimes. They are here, not more than an hour's drive from Bucharest."

As he watched the change of expression in the other man's eyes, he pulled a fresh cigar from a breast pocket and rolled it between his fingers. Now the arrogance pervaded his features.

"Why haven't these jewels already been confiscated?" von Wassner demanded.

"Two reasons. The first, because their owner has been very helpful to our cause. The second reason is because I have deleted all records of them from my reports. Only the family, myself, and Canaris know of their existence."

Von Wassner thought about it. As head of the Abwehr, Admiral Canaris was an honest military man. Unlike Göring, Canaris cared nothing about raping the countries that the Third Reich had conquered.

"Who is the family?" von Wassner asked.

"A very highly placed Romanian family, anti-Bolshevik."

"You have proof of this?"

"I can lead you directly to them."

"I didn't ask you that," von Wassner barked. "Do you have proof?"

Eisling ignored the question. Calmly, he started to light his cigar. Von Wassner brought the barrel of the Luger down across the other man's head, just hard enough to stun but not enough to crush the skull.

"The *proof*, Eisling!"

"The report," Eisling rasped. "I have the only original copy of the report . . . the one I never filed!"

"Where is it? I want to see it."

Von Wassner softened his voice, the way he did when interrogating a prisoner. When no answer came, he hit Eisling again, this time across the temple, harder.

"No!" the man whimpered, falling to his knees, a hand covering the place where von Wassner had struck him.

"Yes, you fat pig! Do you think I would gamble taking you along without knowing you're worth it?"

It was in the Abwehr man's eyes: fear, desperation, survival. He telegraphed the move a full second before he made it. His hand had snaked down to his ankle and come up with a small pistol. As he came out of the chair, von Wassner shot him low in the groin.

Eisling screamed as the blood ran out over his pants. Von Wassner bent down. The man moaned softly in German. He tried to scream again, but it came out as a moan and what sounded like *"Bitte."* Von Wassner placed the gun under his ear. Nearby, a truck rattled over the old cobblestones and a horn blew loud and long. They made so much noise that von Wassner felt the recoil and saw the skull explode more than he heard the shot.

He searched Eisling's pockets and found only his identification and the usual paraphernalia. The man's jacket was hung on a nearby chair. He shredded the lining, and found a thick envelope.

One quick scan of its contents told him that he had struck gold. Or, better yet, a fortune in jewels.

In the rear of the Mercedes, von Wassner, a penlight in his right hand, studied the Romanovsky file.

Prince Valentin Romanovsky had fled from Russia during the Bolshevik revolution. In Romania he married the only surviving heir to the powerful house of Cimpeni, Princess Sophia. While the other royal houses fell to financial ruin after World War I, Romanovsky survived and prospered. The reason for this was the tremendous borrowing power of the merged Romanovsky and Cimpeni family jewels. They were worth millions.

When World War II came along, and Romania became an ally of Nazi Germany, Romanovsky gladly supplied Hitler's military machine with oil from his rich Romanian fields. In return for this, the family's fortunes—including the jewels—remained intact.

Greta Schell read the document over von Wassner's shoulder. By the time she finished she was shaking with excitement. "My God, Graf, millions!" she exclaimed.

He smiled. "And ours for the taking."

"But will Romanovsky have them in the castle?"

"He will," von Wassner replied, "if he is a prudent man and not a fool. Like us, he must have seen the end long ago. He would keep the jewels at hand, just in case."

Von Wassner spread a map of Romania on his lap. He studied it for a moment, and then circled the village of Cernavoda.

"Herr Gruppenführer . . ."

"Ja?"

"The bridge."

A mile ahead lay the Fetesti Bridge across the Danube. On each side they could see the tiny huts of the checkpoint guards.

The driver slowed as they approached the western side of the bridge. No one challenged them from the hut.

"They have probably set up a line on the eastern bank," von Wassner said evenly. "When the Reds come, it will be from there. Drive on."

But they got no challenge on the eastern side of the river either. Von Wassner's antennae came up on full alert. Something was wrong, very wrong. . . .

But it was too late.

Greta Schell saw them first, a Red Army patrol. They materialized from the trees beside the road.

She screamed, but the sound was drowned out by rifle fire.

Sergeant Boris Glaskov was five feet ten. His body under his dirt-brown uniform was broad and solid. His sandy hair was long and limp with perspiration. His brown eyes were flecked with gold and set too close together for most people's taste, including his own.

They made him look cruel, devious, and dishonest. This was a disadvantage, since he *was* cruel, devious, and dishonest. Glaskov was one day past his twenty-first birthday.

He munched a candy bar he had taken from the Mercedes driver's pocket, and examined the watch he had pulled from the man's wrist.

He was angry. The fools had opened fire without his order. The woman was beautiful. They could have all raped her before they killed her. The fools.

A blanket was dropped at his feet. "From the two in the back, Comrade Sergeant."

Glaskov looked up at the man with his dead stare. "What did you keep, Corporal?"

The corporal started to protest, thought better of it, and pulled von Wassner's SS ring from his finger. He dropped it onto the pile and retreated.

Glaskov went through the SS officer's and the woman's belongings. Anything of value went into the pouch on his belt.

The Portuguese passports were interesting. Heinrich and Greta Bolivar, Lisbon.

He picked up the sheaf of official-looking papers with the Abwehr seal.

Boris Glaskov had been born in the tiny village of Vysokoye, near the Russian border. Because of this, he spoke fluent Polish and German, as well as his native Russian.

He read the complete report on Romanovsky, and then read it again. He looked at the marked map, and then picked up the passports once more.

Boris Glaskov was not educated, but he was cunning. All of these items put together meant something.

Vysokoye was a poor village, and the Glaskov clan the poorest of its inhabitants. Boris had stolen to eat almost from the time he could walk. In fact, if the war had not happened, and he had not been conscripted into the army, his fellow villagers or the GPU would probably have lynched him by now.

As far as Boris was concerned, the revolution had done nothing for him or his family. The only difference was that the grain and meat Boris stole was now the state's instead of his neighbor's. That made it even more likely that when he went home he would be hanged that much sooner.

Boris Glaskov did not want to return to Russia.

He had a gut feeling that the papers he now held might solve that problem for him.

"Corporal?"

"*Da,* Comrade Sergeant?"

"Your grid map of the area."

"*Da.*" The corporal trotted over, pulling the map from his pouch.

"How far are we from the village of Cernavoda?"

The corporal calculated quickly. "About six and a half kilometers, Comrade Sergeant."

Glaskov stood and shouldered his rifle.

"We go there."

Castle Cimpeni was perched on a hill that dominated the countryside clear to the Danube. Its battlements and fortifications recalled a history of conquests and internal wars. The village of Cernavoda clung to the side of the hill, and some of the weathervanes atop the little houses reached almost to the level of the castle's terrace.

On this night, with Red Army artillery booming to

the north and east, the castle was ablaze with light.

Behind its three-foot-thick walls, there was controlled chaos. Servants, directed by Princess Sophia herself, hurriedly packed the most essential of the family's belongings.

Surveying it all through sad eyes was Prince Valentin Romanovsky. He was in his middle fifties, wide and powerfully built, with close-cropped, iron-gray hair and square, solemn features. He wore a black overcoat, a black suit, and carried a narrow-brimmed green felt hat in one big hand. His clothes needed pressing, but there was a certain massive dignity about him. A full-length sable coat was draped over his left arm.

"Sophia."

The woman turned and came immediately to his side. She was fifteen years younger than her husband, but strikingly beautiful in the same way he was regally handsome. Her face, considering the circumstances, was remarkably calm.

"Yes, Valentin?"

"It is enough. We can take no more. Where is Sergei?"

"Freeing the animals," she replied. "He doesn't want his horses under the peasant asses of Bolshevik butchers. His words."

They both laughed. And Romanovsky's eyes filled as they gazed at his wife. In her wealth of midnight hair, which she wore loose and well past her shoulders, restrained from clouding her face by a barrette over each temple. In her steady black eyes. In her features, large but perfectly chiseled. And above all in her complexion, which was as utterly white as her hair was utterly black. She made him think of a madonna.

"What is it, my darling?"

"Nothing. Where is little Sophia?"

"In the nursery. She is being readied."

"Go fetch her. We must leave at once."

She was two steps above him on the wide stairwell, when gunfire erupted in the front courtyard. Screams of dying men reached their ears, and suddenly the massive doors were flung wide.

Fifteen-year-old Sergei Romanovsky was flung to the floor where he rolled toward them. He was followed by three Russian soldiers. The one with the sergeant's stripes approached them.

"Prince Romanovsky?"

"Yes."

"Your family?" The man gestured to the boy and the woman.

"Yes. My wife, Sophia. My son, Sergei."

"And these three?" the sergeant said, nodding toward the dumbstruck women.

"Servants," Romanovsky replied.

"And who else is here?"

Romanovsky hesitated only a second. "Only the male servants . . . outside."

"They are all dead," Boris Glaskov said. He turned and shot the three servant women.

Princess Sophia was too shocked to scream. She gasped in terror and clutched her husband's arm. Young Sergei reacted in the same manner, staring in quiet, stunned disbelief.

"Butchers!" Romanovsky hissed.

"That is so you know I will do everything I say I will do," the sergeant stated flatly. "In there, all of you."

Glaskov prodded them into a small study, and turned

to his men. "Tell the others to stand guard outside. You two, search the house."

Glaskov closed and locked the paneled door behind the men. Using drapery cord, he tied the man and boy to chairs. He bound Princess Sophia spread-eagled across a chaise.

When he was finished, he stood before them. "Boy, where are the jewels?" He jabbed his rifle in Sergei's chest.

"He knows nothing," Prince Romanovsky said.

Glaskov turned to the older man. "And you?"

Romanovsky stared at him, his eyes glittering. "What would a peasant like yourself do with jewels?"

Glaskov slapped him three times. "I have very little time, and even less patience. Where are they hidden?"

Romanovsky spat in Glaskov's face. The sergeant turned to Sophia. He wrapped his right hand in the bodice of her dress and ripped it from her body. Within seconds he had stripped her nude.

Romanovsky cried out in rage. Glaskov slapped him again. "Where are they, all of them! And tell me the truth, old man, because I have an itemized list."

"Valentin," Sophia hissed, "tell this pig nothing!"

Glaskov raised his tunic and unbuttoned the front of his trousers. "Where?"

Sweat poured from the prince's face. "What are you going to do?"

"I am going to rape your wife. *Where!*"

Romanovsky took a deep breath. "In the chapel. There is a false back on the rear of the altar."

Glaskov fell forward between Sophia's legs. She cursed him in screams as he entered her.

TWO

The present time

The electric train from Salzburg droned through the storm and sent the snowflakes spinning crazily in its wake, but nothing could prevent their piling on top of the already deep snow. So far, the train had made good time in spite of the whiteness in the high mountain passes. Fortunately, there was still no wind to create the impassable drifts so common to the Tyrol. The air was unbelievably dry, and the snow was light and fluffy. It was as though the great cloud bank, drifting slowly into western Austria, had stopped, hemmed in by the Alps, and now was trying to shake off its tons of snow in order to raise itself high above the peaks that held it captive and drift on again into the heart of Europe and beyond.

Nick Carter gave up staring out the window, and

glanced at his watch. The train would arrive in Kitzbü-
hel in another twenty minutes, a full two hours late because of the storm.

No matter.

The message hadn't specified a time, only a date. It
had come through the usual contact in Paris, and, as
usual, was cryptic: *Very important I see you in person.
Evening of the tenth, my chalet, Kitzbühel. Lorena.*

Lorena was Madame Lorena Zornova. Carter had
met her ten years earlier, in Vienna, through an equally
cryptic message:

*My name is Lorena Zornova. I am a refugee from
Budapest, a defector, if you wish to call it that. I wish,
in the future, to pass information on to you, only you.*

"Why me?" Carter had asked, when they had finally
met.

"Because my contact in the East knows of you and
thinks you can be trusted." To his surprise, she popped
off several operations he had undertaken in Bulgaria,
Romania, Hungary, and Czechoslovakia.

"All right," Carter said, and nodded, "your information is good. What do you want in return?"

"A modest fee, enough to live here in the West."

"That's reasonable. I think it would be no problem."

A contact and drop was set up through Paris. And the
information she provided was good, pure gold. When it
was something really big, Carter would go to her in
person. Some of those meetings had taken place in trop-
ical, exotic locales.

Lorena Zornova was not a young woman but she was
all woman, and exceedingly beautiful. It was only natu-
ral that she and Carter would eventually share more than
information.

But even in bed he had never learned a shred of knowledge about her past. That was a closed book, with only a hint of anything to come.

"One day I will ask you a very big favor. By then you will owe me several big favors. When that day comes, perhaps then you will know the real Lorena."

Carter had never complained. Neither had David Hawk nor AXE. One intelligence coup followed another through the years as a result of her information.

It had been three years since Carter had last seen her in person.

Carrying just a small overnight bag, the Killmaster stepped from the train into blinding snow. He turned left out of the station and into the back streets of the village. The snow seemed to get heavier with each step from a motionless gray sky.

He stopped for a minute and stood at the corner of a narrow street and listened. There was no traffic of any kind, and the absolute quiet was unnerving. The snowflakes gathered on his bare head and coated his eyebrows. He tried to peer through the snowflakes and penetrate the wall of gloom around him, but he couldn't see more than a radius of twenty feet.

He kept walking until he heard music, and then followed the sound until he saw the window with a lighted stein.

Inside, it was warm and practically empty. The bartender was a giant of a man in height, with a girth to match.

"Schnapps," Carter said, and waited until it was poured. "I just got off the train. I need a taxi."

"Hotel, right across the street."

"No, I need to go a way outside the village."

"*Ach*, on a night like this?" He shook his head, seemed to think on it for a moment, and leaned forward. "You'll pay?"

"I'll pay."

Two minutes later, Carter was back on the street heading four houses down for "old Kirchner's." It seemed that Herr Kirchner ran a car-for-hire, and that he was the only one greedy enough to go out on a night like this.

Carter found the house, knocked on the door, and waited.

The door was opened by a short, stout *Hausfrau* with grayish hair. She looked surprised.

"*Ja?* What do you want?" she said.

"Is Herr Kirchner at home, please?" Carter asked with a smile. "I would like to talk with him."

The woman hesitated a moment. "I will see if my husband is awake yet. He works late, you know," she added. "Wait here."

She closed the door and left Carter standing in the snow. It was several minutes before the door opened again and a man stood on the threshold. He was only half dressed. His nightshirt was bulging over his pants. He was dough-faced and shapeless.

He squinted at Carter. "*Ja?*"

Carter explained his needs and the chalet by name without naming its owner.

Kirchner blustered, waved his hands pointing at the falling snow, and in no uncertain terms declared that Carter was crazy.

The Killmaster held up an American hundred-dollar bill. The man snatched it and pointed to a vintage, open Jeep at the curb. "Wait."

Carter chuckled to himself as he swept the seat with his hand. If anyone from the other side was keeping track of Lorena Zornova's visitors, he thought, he was leaving a trail a mile wide.

Carter managed to step from the Jeep even though his legs were frozen. The last of the great foul-weather Grand Prix drivers, Hans Kirchner, roared off just as Carter rescued his bag.

He managed to wade through the thigh-high snow-drifts and ring the bell of the chalet. She must have seen the Jeep arrive because the door opened at once.

"I didn't think you'd make it." Her voice was low, husky, and the words came out as if Garbo had announced that she vanted to be alone.

"Some of me didn't, I think," Carter muttered. "I'm frozen."

Lorena laughed. "You should have dressed warmer."

"Lorena, are you going to leave me standing out here all night?"

"Sorry."

She stepped aside and he entered the hallway. The door slammed and she took his coat. Her lips brushed his cheek.

"Good to see you."

"Brandy, woman," he growled. "Now."

"This way."

Carter followed her down the hall and into a small sitting room, cozy, with a roaring fire. He watched her pour brandy into two large snifters.

She looked good.

Did he expect three years would change her appearance? Not Lorena. Her face was a little grave, there were shadows of fatigue beneath her eyes, and she had gained a pound or two, maybe. But she was still the same.

The thick blond hair spilled down from her head over her shoulders, every lock shining and in place. The contours of her face were soft and delicate, the skin pale and clear. The mouth was a red banner across her face, unfurling at the lower lip in a gentle pout.

The dress she wore was of softest wool with a gently draped back. It molded itself lingeringly to her ample curves, then flared slightly so that it swirled as she walked.

"You're staring," she said as she handed him one of the snifters.

"Don't I always?" he shot back with a grin. "*Salud.*"

They touched glasses and sipped the brandy. Carter shivered and moved to the fire. She sank into a vast, pillow-bedecked sofa, the crossing of her legs a whisper of sound.

Carter again raised his glass. "Old times," he said.

"And old faces," she replied.

"Change that old to familiar and I'll drink to it."

She laughed. "You look much nicer when you smile."

They drank.

She put down her glass and took a cigarette from a black lacquer box on the coffee table, offering him one. He got them lighted with very little shaking of numb hands and sat down.

Lorena studied him. "I'll guess you've taken on about a pound a year," she said. "Three pounds."

"Eight," he replied. "Pounds, that is."

"Otherwise," she continued, "you don't look much different. Except in the eyes. Mature? Grave?"

"Cynical."

Immediately her face closed. "Yes, aren't we all."

"You want to tell me why the hell you dragged me across the Alps in a blizzard?"

"Must I, right now?" she replied, making a face.

"You wanted to see me *right away*, remember?"

"Yes," she sighed. "But you haven't even bothered to kiss me hello."

Carter cocked his head to one side. "This doesn't sound like Lorena Zorkova."

"No, it doesn't . . ."

"But—" He shrugged, and leaned forward to brush his lips across hers. "There."

"Christ, Nick," she groaned, "you're so damn romantic."

"I know. Speak to me."

She crushed her cigarette in an ashtray, fell back on the sofa, and closed her eyes. "It's a long story, Nick. It starts in 1944. I was just a year old." She paused and opened her eyes to stare at him for a second. "Now you know I'm a middle-aged woman."

"You're being coy again."

"Sorry." She smoothed her dress and shifted her position. "Of course, my real name isn't Zorkova."

"I never thought it was," Carter replied.

"Have you ever heard the name Romanovsky?"

"Several times. It's a common Russian name. We probably have two hundred Romanovskys in our files."

"Prince Valentin Romanovsky?"

Carter thought for several minutes, then shook his head. "No, but that wouldn't be unusual. After the revolution, there were damn few princes around."

A smile curled her lips and her eyes narrowed to slits. "So true. Prince Valentin Romanovsky was my father. Princess Sophia of Romania was my mother. I also have a brother, Sergei."

"*Was*, and *have*?" Carter said, his brow furrowing in curiosity.

"My brother is still alive. My parents are dead. That's where the story begins . . ."

For the next hour, Carter sat transfixed as she told him the events of that evening so many years before. He didn't move until she paused. Then he took her glass, liberally filled it and his own, and resumed his seat.

"What happened then, after the Russian sergeant raped your mother?"

"My father went mad. The Russian left the room. By then his two men had searched the house. They hadn't found me in the upstairs rooms. When the shooting started, my nurse hid both of us on top of the canopy above my bed."

Here she paused and took a long drink of brandy. Carter lit fresh cigarettes for them both and let her take her time.

"My bedroom had two doors, one into the hall, the other directly into the family chapel. We saw the sergeant remove the jewels from the rear of the altar. He brought them into the bedroom and carefully compared them to a list he had. When he seemed satisfied, he hid the jewels in his clothing and built up some twigs and papers in the fireplace. He was about to light it, when two soldiers appeared in the doorway. He asked them if it was done. Both of them nodded. Then he killed them, both of them. He sprayed both of them with his rifle, his own comrades."

"You remember all this so clearly?" Carter asked.

"Not really. I was only a baby, and by then my nurse,

Nanya, was covering me with her body to make sure I wouldn't cry out. But later, I heard every detail many, many times."

"Go on," Carter said.

"The Russian dropped a match to start the fire, and then bolted from the room. Nanya dropped to the floor and rushed to the fireplace. For years after that, she told us that she never really knew why she saved the papers the Russian was trying to burn. Something just told her to do it."

"What were they?"

"I'll get to that. There was more shooting from the front courtyard. Nanya rushed to the window. The Russian sergeant had killed his other two comrades. Nanya watched him ride off in the sleigh that was supposed to have taken us to the sea."

"And your parents? Your brother?"

She continued as if Carter hadn't spoken. "We waited in the bedroom for nearly an hour before going downstairs. My brother was babbling, but Nanya got the story out of him. The two soldiers had come into the room right after the sergeant had left. One of them shot my mother and father. He was turning his gun on my brother, when the other soldier stopped him.

"He shouted in Russian that he would not be a party to the killing of children. The other soldier just shrugged and they left the room, letting my brother live."

Suddenly she stood. "As you can tell, all of this is very depressing for me. There are three things I need when I am depressed . . . drink, food, and sex. We have had drink. Now I will make us some sandwiches. I'll be right back."

She returned in no time with a tray of food and two

bottles of good Romanian lager. They ate in silence, Carter mulling over the story thus far, and not hiding his curiosity to hear the rest of it.

At last she pushed her plate away and continued.

"Nanya hitched horses to another sleigh. She bundled the two of us into it and headed north, into the mountains. She knew the countryside well. We were able to avoid the retreating Germans and the advancing Russians. In two days' time we reached her village, Vailia, near the Russian border."

"And obviously survived," Carter murmured.

"Oh, yes, thanks to Nanya. Vailia was a partisan village. Nanya's family accepted us without question. We were given the identity cards of two children of neighboring families who had recently died."

"So you grew up in Vailia?" Carter said.

"Yes. I became Lorena Zorkova."

"And your brother?"

"Sergei became Vadim Vinnick."

Carter paused with the bottle of lager halfway to his lips.

Vadim Vinnick was the all-powerful head of the Romanian intelligence service.

Carter stood under the shower, letting the hot water finish thawing the cold from his bones.

In his mind he went over every word of Lorena Zorkova's story. At first he had thought it farfetched. Then, when she had gotten to the kicker, the punch line, he found himself wanting to believe every word.

"My brother wants to meet with you, face-to-face."

"That could be tricky, in Romania," Carter had replied.

"He knows that. You can get into Hungary unnoticed?"

"Yes."

"Then he can get you into Romania."

"Great. Why?"

"I'm afraid he will have to tell you that. Remember, many years ago I told you that one day I would require a favor?"

"Yeah, I remember."

He had stalled, but he knew he would go. Somehow it seemed to be in the cards. And, besides, if he met face-to-face with a man as high up as Vadim Vinnick and got back out, it had to prove profitable.

He dried his body, wrapped a towel around his hips, and entered the bedroom. Lorena was stretched across the bed. The lights had been dimmed and she had changed into something sheer and feminine.

He remembered her earlier comment. "I hope you're still depressed," he quipped.

She laughed, a light, ringing sound in the still room. "Yes, very depressed."

She slid from the bed and Carter closed the distance between them. When he kissed her she did nothing at first, neither responding nor withdrawing. Then Carter put his arms around her, bringing her close, and she snatched out at him with surprising passion, pulling him to her and forcing herself against him. They parted finally, both breathless.

"I am glad my brother contacted me when he did. You see, I wanted to see you myself. I feel like a nun in this village." Her voice was low, husky, full of unmasked desire.

She came forward, kissing him again, but more gently

this time, without the former urgency. When it was over, she stepped away from him, breathing heavily.

She took the wispy gown and pulled it slowly up over her thighs and hips, and then slid it over her head, all in one easy movement.

She was nude except for a tiny piece of cloth on her hips. The thighs were downy-soft, the sweep of curve from hip to waist was stunning, the breasts were ripe and inviting. She smiled at him, her eyes heavy-lidded, her mouth partly open.

"Well?" she breathed.

Carter grabbed her and pulled her against him, and then they were kissing again, his mouth exploring her hot one, his hands finding the beautiful curves of her flesh.

She pulled away, gasping for breath, her eyes slightly glazed over now, her body trembling gently. "Take me," she murmured.

She fell to the bed. Carter discarded the towel and joined her. He found her seeking tongue, and the golden thighs, and the hot flesh of her body pressed insistently against him.

She took his hand and put it where she wanted it to be, around her breasts first, where she left it for a long time, her eyes half closed and her breathing becoming heavy, and then down, parting for him.

He manipulated her with his fingers and then moved his head downward. With a cry she raised her hips to meet him.

"Harder, yes, harder!" she cried out, bucking and groaning under his lips.

Then she pulled him up over her. She was wetly ready, sighing as he entered her. At the beginning they both stopped for a moment, resting briefly, and then started again in perfect time, unhurried. She was slightly ahead, moving faster, urging him on at the very last.

He strained to catch her, and did, so that they exploded together. She screamed out and clutched at him, burying her face into his shoulder and murmuring, "Oh, oh!" over and over again.

He awoke first, morning giving broad shapes and forms to the trees outside the window, deep grays with touches of white, as though they were part of a giant canvas. He looked across at Lorena. She lay on her side, facing him. The sheet had slipped down to reveal her left breast, beautifully round, deeply full, the delicate pink circle tipping it. He swung from the bed, went into the bathroom, showered and shaved, and dressed. She was awake when he came out, sitting up with the sheet wrapped around her.

"Sleep well?" He smiled affably at her.

"Quite," she replied, and grinned.

"I've got a scrambler device with me. I'll call Washington."

"And tell them what?" she asked.

"That I'm going over."

He wasn't sure as he turned away, but he thought her smile was just like the one on the cartoon cat that ate the canary.

THREE

Carter caught the early-morning train out of Kitzbü-hel and arrived in Salzburg before noon. He checked the schedules and found he had forty minutes before the express to Vienna pulled out.

There were two ranks of pay telephones, one at each end of the terminal. He idled by one bank of phones until he had a number, and then walked across the terminal. He dropped the required coins in the slot and waited until a husky female voice answered with the number he had just dialed.

"Tell Gunter that an old friend wants to talk to him," Carter said. "The number is Salzburg 779-101."

He hung up and walked leisurely across to the other bank of phones.

No one paid him any attention.

He waited nearly five minutes in the booth before the phone rang. "Yes?"

27

"All my old friends have died from bad drink and loose women. Who is this?"

"Gunter, you fat old thief. I'm glad to hear they haven't shot you on the other side for short-changing and overcharging."

"How could they?" replied the gravelly voice in barely accented English. "I am the answer to their black-market prayers. I haven't heard from you in an age. You must want something."

"I have to go over," Carter said, "and I don't want to be made."

"When?" The voice suddenly got serious.

"Tonight, if possible."

"That might be arranged. You're in Salzburg?"

"Yes. I'll arrive in Vienna around seven."

"Should be enough time. Take a taxi from the station out to my country place. You remember it?"

"I do."

"I'll try to have everything ready."

Carter hung up, bought a paper, and boarded his train.

He had a light lunch in the dining car and slept fitfully all the way to Vienna.

The snow had turned to a light rain, making the streets of the old city glisten. Clutching his light bag, he ignored the taxi queue outside the station and walked several blocks before hailing a passing cab.

"Where?"

"The country. I'll direct you."

In no time they had left the city. The windshield wipers flicked steadily. They drove past stolid-looking houses surrounded by stone walls and dripping trees. The streets were as silent as the hills that rolled behind them. Eighteen miles out of the city they exchanged the highway for a mountain road that climbed up through dripping fir trees to a sodden expanse of pastureland. The farmhouses were dark and isolated. Dogs barked as the headlights lit the barns and outbuildings.

They had climbed another three miles, when a building loomed out of the mist, fields stretching behind it into wet darkness.

"Here," Carter growled.

The driver braked. The headlights shone on a wooden chalet surrounded by an ugly wall built of stone and iron piping. Water ran from the gutters. The shutters were closed. Not a single light showed. Carter gave the driver his shillings and added a large tip.

"Thanks for your trouble."

The man pocketed his money, glanced across at what looked like a deserted chalet, and drove off.

Carter walked around to the rear and opened a gate in the stone wall. He could see light in the first-floor-rear room, mostly obscured by heavy curtains. He waited a minute or two before crossing a patch of broken concrete and then onto a stretch of lawn.

Interesting, he thought. Gunter Forbin was probably worth millions, yet his "country house" was little more than a dump. But then, when one made one's millions by not paying duty on Western goods smuggled into Eastern bloc countries, it didn't pay to advertise one's wealth.

The ground sloped down and there were steep steps to the basement. The opaque glass door was open as promised. Carter stepped into the passage; there was a wedge of light at the far end. As he moved, the light widened until the whole of the far end was illuminated and Gunter stood silhouetted like a giant against the far wall.

"It's me," Carter said.

"I know," came the reply with a peal of laughter, "I could hear your catlike stealth from the grave. Come in, I have schnapps."

The room was plain. Carter supposed that the two doors leading off were to a bedroom and kitchen. There was a new armchair, and a table pushed into a corner looked new. There wasn't much else. Photos of impossibly structured nude women hung from walls badly in need of paint and plaster.

The Killmaster took the offered tumbler of schnapps and set his bag on the table. "You really should spend some of your money, Gunter," he said with a grin, making a face as he surveyed the room.

"Oh, but I do, I do!" the big man roared. "In Paris, Rome, New York! But not here. Here, I am a poor man. *Prosit!*" He drank and wiped his mustache with his fingers.

"What have you got for me?" Carter asked, draining his own glass.

"You have my fee, of course?"

"Of course," Carter replied, withdrawing an envelope from his jacket and dropped it in the big man's lap. "There's a little extra in there. I'll need a few things on the other side."

"No problem." As if by magic, a passport and a fist of papers appeared on the table in front of Carter. "For the time you are there, you are Emil Bunder, a relief lorry driver. I used one of your photos from the last time. Here is your union permit, your driver's license, and your visa for three days of holiday. I assume your business will take no longer than that?"

"Let's hope not. I'm going over in a lorry?"

Gunter Forbin nodded. "As a relief driver. You're in luck. I have a shipment going over legally at midnight . . . seed and packaged manure."

"In the dead of winter?" Carter said.

The big man shrugged. "My Communist customers like to look ahead."

"What's under the seed and shit?"

Forbin grinned. "Perfume, cosmetics, blue jeans, rock and roll tapes . . . just more shit. Come along, my friend, and we'll wardrobe you."

From a closet and drawers in the bedroom, Carter outfitted himself from the skin out in used, locally labeled clothing. The pants and shirt were worn denim, and the old fur-collared leather jacket was cracked with age.

"What will you need over there?" Forbin asked.

"I'm going skiing. Everything should be used. Oh, and a gun . . . something local to the country."

Forbin nodded. "Check into the Pension Galpi, on Lenin Korut. It will all be waiting. Will you be shooting anyone?"

"I hope not," Carter said.

"Then you won't need extra clips. What about wheels?"

"I'll rent a car there."

"Good. Let's have another schnapps and talk about women."

An hour later, a knock came on the rear door and Forbin admitted a man nearly his own size, with long, lank black hair and a simian forehead that practically covered his eyes.

His name was Klaus, and he would drive the lorry over.

There was little traffic on the main road east out of Vienna to the frontier, much less than Carter had hoped for. It would be a lot easier to move across a busy frontier than a deserted one. Most of the traffic was trucks. Carter hoped they would blend in and he passed across like so many ants.

About two miles from the border, the trees disappeared and the road narrowed. A little farther on, they slipped into a long line and moved forward in fits and starts.

"How long does this usually take?" he grumbled.

Klaus shrugged. He was a man of no words. He hadn't said one since they had left Gunter Forbin's chalet.

Eventually they reached the Austrian barrier. The bills of lading were scarcely glanced at and they were waved through.

The second barrier, into Hungary, was a different story. The two trucks ahead were surrounded by a score of armed border guards. Carter glanced across at Klaus, hoping for some sign of assurance, some indication that that number of guards was not unusual. He was hunched forward, his thick arms crossed on the steering wheel, staring straight ahead. His phlegmatic expression said nothing.

The thin arm of a wooden barrier lifted and the first truck moved slowly ahead. Carter would have given a year's earnings to have been sitting in that truck. Klaus eased forward a length and pulled on the brakes and switched off his engine. The guards in greatcoats and fur hats watched them approach incuriously, their hands dug deep into their pockets, their rifles slung from shoulder straps. When the lorry stopped, they sauntered toward it.

Klaus buttoned up his leather jacket, opened the door, and with a short, curt "*Kommen*," stepped out. Carter climbed down his side and the guards moved back to give him room. Klaus strode stolidly toward the large building constructed of rough-cut, unpainted planks. Carter tailed along behind him.

A guard at the door nodded to Klaus and greeted him by name. Inside, there were four civilians standing behind a counter and an officer in a gray-green uniform sitting at a desk behind them, reading a newspaper. Klaus unfolded his manifest and stacked the truck's papers and his passport on top of it.

One of the civilians turned them around and began to check the documents. Carter took out his phony passport and, matching Klaus's brusque manner, dropped it onto the counter, then turned and looked the place over with a nonchalance he was far from feeling.

Two men, apparently the crew of the first truck, were slouched over the counter a few feet away, patiently waiting for their clearance. They glanced at Klaus, but they didn't speak.

The man checked everything including the fine print in Klaus's papers, then carried them over and laid them on the desk of the officer. He glanced at them casually, hammered the manifest with a rubber stamp, and turned back to his newspaper. Carter's blood pressure went down another few degrees . . . despite the tense buildup, this was a routine crossing.

The civilian gave Klaus his documents and picked up Carter's passport, fingered it open, and glanced at him with flat blue eyes. "Where's Foss?" he asked.

"What?"

"The regular man, Foss? Where is he?"

The uniformed officer looked up and frowned. Carter did the same toward Klaus.

"Drunk," Klaus said, and shrugged. "I wasn't going to take a relief driver, but Bunder here wanted to take his holiday in Budapest."

By this time, the officer was on his feet examining Carter's passport. "Three days? Where will you stay in Budapest?"

"Galpi, the Pension Galpi on Lenin Korut."

"Wait."

He crossed the room to a telephone. He had to dial three times in order to find the right person. When he did, he talked for a full three minutes, scowling now and then at Carter.

Finally he returned and tossed the passport on the counter. "*Ja*," he said, and returned to his paper.

Outside, Carter said in a low voice, "Was that usual?"

"No," Klaus grunted, and climbed up into the cab.

Great, Carter thought, *just great*.

A few seconds later the barrier was raised and they were on the road to Budapest.

Well, I'm in. Now the trick will be to get back out when the time comes!

• • •

The Pension Galpi was in the old part of Buda, close to the Danube and the downtown section. But it was also remote, in that it seemed a town within a town, bearing little resemblance to the newer part of the city. The streets were narrow, most of them cobblestoned.

"You have a reservation, mein Herr?"

"*Ja*," Carter replied, pushing his passport across the desk toward the concierge, a gaunt man with wavy yellow hair.

The man took one look at the name on the passport, and a key appeared from beneath the desk. "Number Seven, second floor, rear."

He turned away as if he were afraid he would catch something, and Carter headed for the stairs.

The room was small, neat and clean. Piled in the center of it was Carter's gear, all used with local labels, just as he'd asked for. It took him fifteen minutes, but he finally found the gun, a Frommer 7.65 Stop Model 19. The seven-shot clip in the butt was full. Carter put it back in the heavy lining of the ski parka, undressed, and fell into the bed.

He slept the sleep of the dead until just after ten, and called around for a car until eleven. An hour later, he picked it up and parked in front of the pension. In no time he was packed and on the road north.

It had stopped snowing, but the fresh wind, which was breaking up the clouds, also whipped up the snow, kiting it crazily into drifts. All the way to Hatvan he could see snowplows in action on the main and secondary roads.

Just north of Hatvan the road began to climb into the Bukk Mountains. It was there that Carter spotted the tail. It was a small, two-door Volga sedan, black, with one occupant.

In the village of Nearing, he stopped for lunch. The Volga raced on by before he could get a good look at the driver or get a read on the plate number.

Over pork smothered in onions, Carter tried to reason it out. Lorena's instructions to him from her brother were clear and precise. He would have to enter Hungary on his own. From Budapest he should drive northeast into the Bukk Mountains. There, he should check into the Cozamor ski resort, where he would be contacted.

By whom?

That would be determined by Vinnick at the last minute. If possible, he would come into Hungary to meet Carter. If not, a way would be found to get Carter over the Romanian frontier.

Just before Eger, Carter saw the Volga fall in behind him again. This time the car was close enough to spot the driver, a very pretty blonde somewhere in her twenties.

Just to make sure, Carter speeded up. The blonde speeded up. When he slowed, she slowed.

Well, Vinnick, it's your move, Carter thought, and then took a deep breath. *At least I hope this move is yours!*

FOUR

The Cozamor Lodge was a sprawling, attractive-looking place nestled against the backdrop of snow-covered mountains and black forests.

Carter took a turn around the parking lot before heading for the entrance. There were several two-door Volga sedans, several black, so it was impossible to tell if the blonde—who had disappeared somewhere in the village below—had preceded him.

There was valet parking, and the young man informed Carter that all his gear and bags would be delivered to his room.

Inside, a sloe-eyed beauty behind the reception desk gave Carter a nice smile, a room key, and copied down all the details from his passport. Two bellmen appeared with his belongings and led him through a maze of corridors.

The cell-like people's luxury room had bare, unpainted cement walls, a single, narrow bed, a chair, a washbasin, and sound-deadening wall-to-wall rubber matting on the floor.

Carter tipped the two bored bellmen and succeeded in wrestling the window up an inch to let out some of the stiflingly excessive heat.

He built a drink from a bottle in his bag, and shaved. At seven sharp, sporting a change of clothes, he walked back out to the lobby. He was passing the desk, when the girl with the sloe eyes called out to him.

"Herr Bunder, there is a message for you."

She handed him a small white envelope. The alias, Emil Bunder, was scrawled across the front of it along with his room number. The hand was definitely feminine, and the flap was tightly sealed.

He tore it open. The message, in the same hand, read, *I am in the bar.*

Carter turned to the receptionist. "Who left this?"

"I really don't know, mein Herr," she replied with a shrug. "I was in the rear at the switchboard, and when I returned it was here on the counter."

"*Danke.*"

He pocketed the envelope and the note and moved on through the lobby. At the entrance to the disco, he paused and glanced inside.

The music blasted through the small, darkened room, amplified by several hundred watts of electronic equipment. The crowd was varied, men in suits and ties and women in clinging dresses, dancing hip to hip with young boys in jeans and child-women in tight sweaters and unbelievably tight stretch pants.

Carter couldn't spot the Volga-driving blonde, and

moved on through the nearly empty dining room into the bar.

There were three men at the bar and two others at a nearby table. But what caught Carter's eye was the woman who sat alone at a table next to the windows. She must have just come in because she still had snow in her dark brown hair. She was wearing dark corduroy slacks and a short leather jacket.

She glanced up just as Carter stepped through the door. Her eyes seemed to leap at him from clear across the room. He was about to move forward, when he suddenly spotted color and movement out of the corner of his left eye.

The color was red, a matching sweater and slacks outfit. The movement was the Volga-driving blonde.

She curled an arm around Carter's neck and came up on her toes to kiss him lightly on the lips. "Emil, you got my note," she breathed. "Over here, I already have a table."

Carter darted a last quick look at the brunette, and followed the blonde with a light sigh. He had almost made a very real blunder.

You will be contacted, Lorena had said.

He had almost tried, mistakenly, to do the contacting.

He moved around the table and held the chair for the blonde. She sat down, and he found himself staring down over her shoulder. It was quite a view. A long mane of honey-blond hair and firm, full breasts filling the front of the sweater.

There was a carafe of wine and two glasses already on the table. She poured as Carter took the opposite chair.

"Since we're such old friends," he murmured, "you'd better give me a name to call you."

"Jarvia."

"And you drive a black Volga sedan," he said, taking the envelope and a pen from his jacket pocket.

"I did today, all the way from Budapest. I almost contacted you at the pension, but decided to wait until you got here."

"Oh?"

"Yes. What's this?" she asked, as he slid the envelope and pen across the table toward her.

"Would you mind writing on that? Something like, 'I am in the bar.'"

Her smile was magic, wide with white, gleaming teeth, as were her eyes, blue and bright. "Of course." She wrote. Carter checked it against the note. They matched perfectly. "Satisfied?"

"For now," he replied. "When do we go skiing?"

"We don't have to. He is here, close by. Go to your room and get a coat. Meet me just over the hill there, beyond the tennis courts." She nodded her head to the window.

Carter followed her gaze and saw a swimming pool covered for the winter, and a line of snow-covered tennis courts surrounded by tall fences.

"There is a path just beyond the courts," she continued. "Follow it to the top of the hill. I'll meet you there."

He leaned forward and lowered his voice. "Just whom am I meeting?"

"Still testing me?" The toothpaste-ad smile hadn't left her face.

"Just answer the question."

The table was mirror-topped. She bent forward and breathed hard on it. Then she printed with the tip of one finger: *VADIM VINNICK*.

Carter erased it with his sleeve, and stood. "Five minutes."

The lane was steep and icy in spots. It was also narrow, with mid-grown fir trees lining the way. Every fifty yards or so there was a dim yellow light mounted on a pole.

About halfway up, she stepped from the shadows of two trees. She wore a knee-length fur coat now with a white scarf knotted at her throat.

"There is a road at the view-top leading down the other side. I left my car up there."

She started off, and Carter stopped her with his voice. "Where are we going?"

"To Lillafored. It's about—"

"I know where it is," he replied curtly. "Isn't a teeming village a little dangerous for a meeting like this?"

For the first time, the beauty-pageant smile disappeared and her lips became a tight line across her face. "I have my orders. I only do as I am told."

"How close are you to Vinnick?"

She tried to smile again, but it was a weak effort. "How close can a man and woman get?"

"Then you should be able to tell me who sent me over, shouldn't you?"

Her hesitation was enough. Carter started forward, but stopped when her hands came out of the pockets. Held steady, its barrel not wavering from Carter's chest, was a Rommer exactly like the one under his belt in the center of his back.

"Herr Bunder . . . or whatever your name is . . . I have no time—"

That was all she said. The gun dropped from her hands. Shock filled her face and she pitched forward into the snow.

The only sound had been two muffled pops like champagne corks coming out of their bottles. The sound had been very near, somewhere in the darkness of the trees.

The woman had barely hit the ground when Carter dived back into the shadow of the trees, dragging his own gun into the clear.

"If you are armed, don't shoot. I will show myself," came a voice from the shadows.

"You do just that," Carter hissed.

The tall brunette in the leather jacket stepped into the light. A silenced revolver dangled from the index finger of her left hand. Her right hand was held far away from her body.

"My name is Ilse Beddick. You are an American agent. Your name is Nick Carter. You were sent here by Lorena Zorkova. This—she nodded at the body on the ground—"is Jarvia Karoly. She is an agent of the Hungarian SSB."

Carter stepped out into the light himself, slipping the Rommer back into his belt.

"Why?" he said.

"They probably saw Vadim and myself slipping across the border last night. They know Vadim has made contacts in the West, but they want proof to unseat him."

"The Hungarians?"

"Vadim will explain it all to you. This one didn't realize that I recognized her. Help me!"

Carter took the shoulders and she the feet. They dragged the lifeless form a good fifty yards off the trail before the brunette called a halt.

"Clear the snow away enough for a grave. There's a maintenance shed down by the tennis courts. I'll be right back."

By the time he had cleared an area down to the ground, she had returned. She was carrying a small spade and two buckets of water. Carter saw the intent at once, and went to work.

Trying to get through the crust was like trying to dig through cement. He had to jam the shovel against it with all his strength and then jump straight-legged on the upper edge. It took him fifteen minutes to break through. The rest was relatively easy going. He dug a pit more than deep enough for the body.

Then, after shoveling the crusty snow in first, he turned and dragged the body to the hole.

"Wait."

Carter watched as the brunette went through the pockets of the fur coat and came up with the keys to the Volga. She also took the blonde's purse. Then she literally kicked the body into the hole.

Carter shook his head. This was one very cold lady.

He shoveled the snow in and stamped it down with his boots. Carefully, he smoothed the top layer with the back of the shovel. He turned to the buckets of water. A thin layer of ice had already formed over the top. He broke it with the shovel and poured the water evenly over the grave. In an hour, the top layer would freeze and it would meld with the rest of the snow.

"Good, that should confuse them for a while."

"What now?" he said.

"I'll get rid of her car. You drop the buckets and the shovel off in the shed."

"And then?" Carter said.

"You're going skiing. Here's a map of the number Two run off the north side. Right about here, there will be a sign on your right, DANGER, TRAIL CLOSED. Take that trail."

He glanced at her. "I take it the trail isn't dangerous?"

She nodded. "I put the sign up myself. I'll meet you halfway down the alternate run, about here."

"Where is Vinnick?" Carter asked.

"In an old farmhouse about two miles farther on. I was not supposed to bring you down until tomorrow night, but they have forced a change in plan."

"Just who are 'they'?"

She started to reply, then stopped. "I think it better that Vadim explain all this to you."

Abruptly, before the Killmaster could ask her anything further, she started up the trail.

Carter picked up the buckets and the spade and started down.

It all fit. Or at least he hoped it did.

The blonde, Jarvia Karoly, had followed him from the Pension Galpi in Budapest. It stood to reason he had been made at the frontier by the SSB officer. That was how the blonde had picked him up.

Ilse Beddick, being with Vinnick, wouldn't know what name he was traveling under, or where he would be staying in Budapest.

He remembered the look on the brunette's face when

he'd walked into the bar. He could see now that it had been a look of recognition. He also remembered the snow in her hair. Obviously she had just entered the bar from the outside. That probably meant that she had just arrived at the lodge.

It fit, he thought.

He just hoped that Vinnick, when they met, could answer the rest of the questions rambling around in his mind.

FIVE

Carter walked along the freshly plowed street toward the lift station. The snow was piled high on the sides, soft and powdery.

At the lift station he was relieved to find he was not the only guest who had decided on a midnight run. There were about fifteen people lined up for tickets.

Carter studied them carefully as he waited in line. They were young, the men tall and athletic, and the women attractive in snug-fitting ski outfits.

Ilse Beddick was not among them.

He got his ticket and walked along the railed corridor toward the cars. Again he looked at the sky. There would be a moon before long, not a full one, but it would be too bright for comfort. He decided to remain in the shadow below the big wooden platform until his number was called. He could hear the shuffling feet and laughter of the people above him. Most of the conversa-

46

tion was in Hungarian, with a sprinkling of German.

Carter waited for the last seat and dropped into it while it was still moving. There was no one behind him, and no one who had gone before him had given him a second glance.

At the top, there was a large sign directing skiers to the five runs and indicating their degree of difficulty.

Carter smiled to himself.

Number Two on the north was by far the most difficult. Ilse Beddick had made a good choice.

To a man and woman, the group in front of Carter fanned out to the easier runs. Carter found himself alone at the top of number Two.

He killed a little time by crouching and coating his skis with oil from a hand roller. When he could hear no more chatter from the others, he discarded the hand roller and poled his way over the precipitous lip.

Then he was plunging downward, gathering speed into the first bank. Startled birds exploded from the neighboring pines as he accelerated. He felt the exhilaration of taking the course as fast as he could. A line of trees came up quickly, a flat area unexpectedly dark, shielded from the brightness of the moon.

And he felt ice suddenly under his skis and the sudden burst of speed that came with it. His legs bent lower and he felt the pull on his thigh muscles. The jump, as it came up, was not so high as it was unexpectedly fast, and he made a mental note of it. He sailed into the air, came down on a flat slope that immediately became a traverse of steep bumps and rolls. A right turn came at him and he felt soft snow, leaned into it hard, and took it without slowing.

A line of trees again, longer, the shadows deeper,

and hard, blue ice. He saw the green shapes hurtling past as another traverse came up and he went airborne and down, airborne and down again in a twisting path where a single error would mean crashing into the trees and almost certain death.

Coming out of it, the slope flattened, rose, and went into a long schuss that looked deceptively simple as he gathered speed only to find it dotted with bumps and rolls.

Then he saw the sign and leaned into a hard right turn that sent powder swirling in a twenty-foot arc.

The alternate trail was narrower and the snow softer, slowing his descent.

In seconds he saw her figure on a rise in front of him. When she was sure it was Carter, she turned and sped off. He fell in behind. Not more than two minutes later, she left the trail and wove dangerously through the trees.

Carter had to admire her skill. It was all he could do to keep up with her, and his heart was pounding like a trip-hammer.

Then he saw the farmhouse, light in the downstairs windows. It was steep-roofed and loomed large in the moonlight.

The woman slid to a halt and Carter came up beside her. They unbuckled their skis and mounted the steps to the porch. Carter expected some kind of watchdog, and when no one appeared, commented on it.

"Too risky," she replied. "Only the two of us know about this meeting. Come this way."

He followed her around to the side of the house. She rapped twice on a pair of French doors, and they entered a large, cozy room heated by roaring logs in a huge fireplace.

In a rocker by the fire was a gaunt man beneath a lap robe. His face was a sickly, sallow color, and his tangle of wiry gray hair was an invitation for nesting birds. He was approaching his sixtieth birthday, but he looked an ailing twenty years older than that.

When he looked up, his eyes were dark and cavernous, but they were also alert, and they assessed all of Carter in one penetrating look.

"Ah, Carter. Please sit down. You'll forgive my rudeness at not standing. I must conserve as much strength as possible. You see, I am dying."

Ilse Beddick poured tea for herself and Vinnick, and found brandy for Carter. As she did this, she related the night's events at the lodge.

"Yes, when I heard you outside, I figured that there had been difficulties. You see, Carter, there are factions in my country, indeed in my own service, who would dearly love to bring me down."

"I guessed as much," the Killmaster replied. "But why?"

"I shall get to that, soon," Vinnick said. "In the meantime, how much did my sister tell you? Oh, by the way, if you wish to smoke, please do. Ilse, find him an ashtray."

Carter eased into Lorena Zorkova's story and speeded up, hitting just the high points as he came to the end. He thought the man had fallen asleep, but when he finished, Vinnick's head came up and his eyes were as bright and penetrating as before.

"Good," he murmured. "When the Soviets moved in

to establish the Communist party, I joined immediately."
Here he paused, a raspy laugh escaping his lips. "I was,
you might say, a ruthless, devoted advocate of the new
regime."

"And you became one of its most powerful and
feared men," Carter offered. "Why?"

"Two reasons . . . survival, and revenge. Now, an answer to your earlier question. I was one of the men who
advocated against complete submission to Moscow. To
do that, we aligned ourselves with Red China as much
or more than with the Kremlin. Because of this, Romania still has some degree of independence."

A little bell went off in Carter's head. "All the information you passed to us through your sister?"

"Exactly. Astute of you at last. All of it was a detri-
ment to the other Eastern bloc countries and Moscow.
That in itself was a form of revenge for what the Bol-
sheviks did to my father. My sister was my eyes and
ears in the West, as well as my conduit to you. The
operation has worked quite well. It has also given my
sister a better life in the West. Ilse, more tea, please."

The woman was at his side at once. Carter studied
the two of them. There was obviously a great deal of
warmth and affection there. Vinnick sensed Carter's
look, and smiled.

"The nurse, Nanya? Ilse is her daughter. When the
time comes, Ilse will join my sister in the West."

"I take it, then," Carter said, "that because of your
health, our little operation is about over?"

"You are quite right. That is why I sent for you. I
wish, for a favor, to put into your hands, Carter, one
very large bulk of information. I am sure that your peo-

ple know that for years the Bulgarians have been putting assassination teams into the West?"

Carter nodded. "It's part of the KGB's system to take international heat off them. The Bulgarians are more than happy to become Moscow's First Directorate trigger people."

"Yes, quite so," Vinnick said, nodding. "There is a large segment of the Bulgarian Dajnavna Sigurnost who revel in creative killing. I have the assumed names, occupations, and addresses of each and every team."

It was all Carter could do to maintain his even expression and his relaxed position in the chair. Already the Bulgarian secret police had pulled off too many political assassinations in the West. It was known that when Moscow wanted someone out of the way, the Bulgarians did the work.

Information of this magnitude would be invaluable. He knew that Washington would go for it at any price.

The Killmaster kept his voice calm. "And the favor?"

The penetrating eyes gazed steadily at Carter. "The night we fled, when Nanya rescued those papers the Soviet sergeant tried to burn?"

"I remember," Carter said.

"I kept those documents all these years. Eventually, by digging through old Nazi records, Russian files, and current computer records, I was able to piece everything together..."

Carter listened to it all, his admiration for the older man's tenacity growing with each word.

Two of the documents belonged to an SS officer and his secretary. They were found in an ambushed car with their driver. Another document was the military identification of the sergeant who had led that Russian patrol,

Boris Glaskov. And there was one more passport. It was Portuguese, identifying one Greta Bolivar.

"Over the years, I dug and dug. I think that Graf von Wassner was on the way to steal my family's jewels that night. I think he was intending to run, but was ambushed by a Russian patrol under the command of Sergeant Boris Glaskov."

"And Glaskov went after the jewels himself," Carter offered.

"Exactly. And when he got them, he destroyed his own papers."

"That left the Bolivar passport."

Vinnick nodded. "It took me years to backtrack the name. Greta Kraussen was an Abwehr agent in Lisbon during the war. She married Heinrich Bolivar in 1942. Because Bolivar's mother was German, Greta enlisted him in the cause. In 1943, they both disappeared. Their disappearance was reported by their contact officer at that time, one Graf von Wassner."

"He killed them himself and kept the passports."

Vinnick nodded. "I believe so. I also think Glaskov escaped to Lisbon with Heinrich Bolivar's passport. But for years I could not trace a Heinrich Bolivar. Then I got a break. About two years ago, I came across this." The frail fingers passed across a dog-eared magazine to Carter.

Carter thumbed through the pages. It was turned to an article about mountain rebels in Uruguay. It seems the rebels had come across the border into Argentina and kidnapped three wealthy ranchers and businessmen. The three men had been rescued, and the leaders of the rebel group were hanged.

There was a photograph of the three men.

Vinnick pointed a shaky finger at the man in the center of the picture. "His name is Enrique Bolivar."

Carter glanced up. "Enrique is Spanish or Portuguese for Henry."

"Or, in German, Heinrich." Vinnick smiled. "It took a great deal more sleuthing, but I found the application for name change and a new passport in the records of a small village in the Algarve. Enrique Bolivar is Boris Glaskov."

Carter took his time replying. "He seems to have done rather well."

"Quite well, with my family fortune. He has been selling the jewels off one by one over the years to support the building of a sizable empire in Portugal and Argentina."

Carter glanced from the magazine to Vinnick. "And now you want revenge."

Vinnick sat back in his chair with a deep sigh and produced a short, slender cigar. Ilse Beddick was on her feet at once.

"Vadim, the doctors . . ."

He waved her away with a smile, and let Carter light the cigar for him. "Revenge? Perhaps. But more. I have learned a great deal about Glaskov/Bolivar. He was a despicable man the night he had my parents murdered and, in turn, murdered his own comrades. In the years since, he has become an even more despicable man. He deserves to die."

Carter stood and began to leisurely pace the room. "I have killed many times, Vinnick. But I'm not a paid assassin, even for the prize you offer."

"I am dying, Carter," came the measured reply. "When I go, my sister will be alone. As you already know, she is not wealthy. The fees we have charged you for information have not been great."

"You want the jewels," Carter said.

Vinnick nodded. "Many of them have been sold, but even more are left. One gem alone is worth a fortune. It is an enormous ruby, called the Heartstone. Because of its great worth, the Heartstone is the symbol of our heritage. It is the crown jewel of the houses of Cimpeni and Romanovsky. If only that one stone could be returned . . ." He stopped with a shrug.

Carter continued to pace. For what Vinnick was offering, he wasn't asking a great deal. He was sure Washington would go along with the deal.

"Obviously, you have a plan," Carter said at last.

"I do," Vinnick replied at once. "Bolivar is preparing to sell off the rest of the jewels. Through the years, he has been dealing with three men. This is always done through intermediaries. Recently, Bolivar contacted all three of these men. They will be going to Argentina soon to bid on the jewels."

"Why is he selling?" Carter asked.

"Simple. His wealth and his power are solid now. He no longer has need of them as security, and the cash they will bring will secure him even greater power."

"It's logical," Carter agreed. "I assume I will take the place of one of the jewel merchants?"

"Exactly. His name is Fabian Huzel. He lives quietly in Amsterdam. He looks and dresses like a man of meager means, but he is one of a handful of men in the world who could arrange the financing for a buy of this size. Probably a third of the stolen jewels in the world pass through Huzel's hands."

Carter listened as the old man explained how the plan would unfold.

"I assume you have contacts in Amsterdam who could help you make all this happen?"

Carter nodded. "There would be a cost factor, but yes, there are such people."

"Good. One more thing. Lorena will go with you."

There it was. Carter looked from Vadim Vinnick to the woman and back again. No, he wouldn't be required to kill Enrique Bolivar. As soon as they had the jewels, Lorena herself would kill him.

They knew his thoughts, but said nothing.

"All right," Carter said, "I'll do it."

The tension disappeared from the room. Ilse Beddick produced a file on Fabian Huzel, and photographs. She also gave Carter the vast research file that had been amassed on Enrique Bolivar. Together, the three of them went over this material for the next two hours. At that time Vinnick called a halt.

"Needless to say, with my enemies in the Hungarian secret police knowing about you, it will be impossible for you to return to the lodge. You will stay here tonight, and we will continue in the morning."

Ilse nodded. "Tomorrow I will make arrangements to get you safely out of the country," she said.

She showed Carter to a comfortable room on the second floor. Everything he needed was there, even a change of clothes and a razor.

The whole thing looked like one very large setup.

"I think," Carter said, "that you and Vinnick tipped off the Hungarians that an American was coming over."

Ilse smiled. "You are as astute as your reputation says you are."

"What would have happened if I had not agreed to this?"

She shrugged. "Your body would have been turned over to the authorities here after I killed you trying to escape. Good night."

Carter undressed and lay on the bed, but he knew he wouldn't be able to get much sleep.

SIX

The place was called the Rotten Apple, and it smelled worse than its namesake. It was on an alley with no name off Dream Street in one of the worst red-light districts in Hamburg.

They sat at a corner table looking out at the dancers moving frantically on a postage-stamp-size dance floor. The music was loud, pounding the walls, and, Carter was sure, damaging his ears.

Sitting across in a pair of hip-hugger jeans, a purple shirt open to expose his chest, and a pair of Gucci loafers, was Count Otto von Krumm. Otto was somewhere close to forty, claimed to be thirty, and bragged that he hadn't bedded a woman over eighteen for twenty years.

Otto von Krumm's father had been in the SS. He had survived the war with only the family castle near the village of Bundesdorg, on the West German/Netherlands frontier. Eventually the old man had died, still saluting the Fuhrer. He had left young Otto the castle, the grounds around it, and a brilliant criminal mind.

For the first thirty years of his life, Otto had stolen everything he could get his hands on and invested it wisely. When he was rich enough, he retired to become an aging hippie who liked a challenge now and then. Quite often Carter offered that challenge.

Von Krumm leaned over and shouted into Carter's ear. "I like it here."

"I can see that," Carter replied. "Can we talk in front of her?"

The German threw an affectionate arm around the voluptuous blonde who sat beside him, his hand accidentally sliding downward to partially cover a breast.

The blonde smiled at Otto. It was an animal smile, earthy and anticipatory. Carter noted that she didn't have any pupils in her eyes.

Carter tried again. "I said, can we talk in front of her?"

"Of course," von Krumm bellowed, and grinned. "She doesn't speak any English at all. Even her German is terrible. But she has the strongest thighs you have ever seen. They are really quite remarkable. Dear me, look at that. And she seems quite taken with you, Nicholas."

Carter followed his stare toward the knot of dancers on the floor. A couple seemed to have taken up residence right in front of their table.

The man was uninteresting, small and swarthy with a moronic face. But the woman was startling. She was barefoot, with long legs and a hard figure ensheathed in a shimmering lamé dress. Her platinum hair was cut short and contrasted sharply with a deep tan.

Each time the couple made a revolving turn, the woman smiled at Carter and ran her tongue along her lower lip.

"Very nice," von Krumm remarked. "I would look into that if I were you . . . in a manner of speaking, of course." He laughed, a deep, rumbling laugh.

Carter got his lips as close as possible to Otto's ear. "Can we talk?"

"Must we? I assume it concerns money."

"It could."

"Gruesome but necessary, I suppose," von Krumm sighed.

"Somewhere else," Carter insisted.

"Very well, we'll go to my flat." Otto rose and nodded toward the platinum blonde. "Why don't you ask her along? We'll have a little entertainment after we talk business."

"No, Otto."

"Very well, follow us to the flat."

"I have the address," Carter said. "I'll meet you there."

Von Krumm led the way out, holding the blonde by the hand. With one eye Carter was watching the shift of her hips as she moved. With the other eye he was watching the hard-eyed little man leave his platinum-haired dancing partner.

Outside, they turned right. Halfway to the corner, Carter whispered, "When you get to your car, drive around the block and keep circling until you see me in your rearview mirror."

Von Krumm nodded and Carter darted into the alley adjoining the club. He made his way around to the rear and walked into the kitchen. A burly man at the door stood to block his progress. Carter waved a fifty-mark bill in his face and he was waved on in.

The Rotten Apple didn't much care if you paid at the front or the rear for entrance, just that you paid.

He was halfway through the knot of dancers when he saw the platinum blonde on a stool at the end of the bar, alone.

"Hi," he said, moving in beside her, close.

"You," she murmured. "I thought you left." Her accent was Belgian or French.

"I came back. Where's your boyfriend?"

"Boyfriend? Haven't got one yet. You interested?"

"The short, dark little guy with the wilted eyes. Where is he?"

"Don't know, don't care," she said, running her hand over Carter's crotch. "Want to dance?"

"No." Carter laid his hand on the inside of her thigh, squeezed, hard.

"Owww, damn you, that hurts!" she exclaimed.

"It can hurt worse. Who is he?"

"Don't know, I swear. He gave me some marks to dance with him. Said he wanted to dance right by your table. That's it, I swear."

Carter believed her. He peeled off another fifty and stuffed it into her cleavage. "Thanks. I like your hair."

The big one at the rear door just shook his head when Carter exited after so short a time. He moved through the alleys until he was four blocks away, on the street where he had parked the rental car near Otto's Mercedes. Keeping to the shadows, he moved up the street until he was in the same block, then darted into a doorway. He had already spotted the little man slouched behind the wheel of a beige Audi parked at the corner.

A hand dropped on Carter's shoulder and he froze.

"You looking for fun, darling?"

He turned slowly, letting the stored-up air in his lungs escape with a hiss.

She was on the wrong side of forty, with a mask of makeup for a face. She wore a thin, clinging black dress relieved by a string of phony pearls and a leather belt with a big silver *L* on it as a buckle.

"Not fun," he murmured, "but maybe something else."

"What else is there?" she said with a throaty laugh, and stepped forward a little so the dim light from the hallway behind lit her.

She had big, heavy breasts, and she showed them by way of a low vee cut to her dress. Her legs were still good where the short skirt revealed them to the darker panty part of her pantyhose. Her skin was dark, swarthy, and it made her nearly white hair stand out like snow on a black stone.

"I can do you back there, at the end of the hall."

She lifted the skirt. There was no crotch in the pantyhose.

"I'll take a raincheck."

"Raincheck? What the hell is *raincheck*?"

Carter pulled her forward a little. "See that Audi down there, the man behind the wheel?"

"*Ja.*"

Carter told her what he wanted. As he did, he unrolled two more fifties from the wad in his pocket and curled them into her hand. "Okay?"

"Sure, okay. But for another fifty I give you a quick one to boot."

Carter saw von Krumm and his blonde go by. "Just do a number on him. That's enough. And remember— you just forget whatever you see. Go!"

He waited until she was across the street and headed down the block before he moved out himself. He pulled the Rommer and held it at his side as he moved from doorway to doorway.

When the hooker crossed back toward the Audi, Carter dropped into a crouch and moved over the side-walk to the line of parked cars.

The hooker was doing a real number. She had the short skirt balled around her waist, the merchandise pumping through the open window practically in the guy's face.

"What are you, cheap?" she was taunting.

"Get lost, whore."

"Who you calling whore . . ."

All of it took no more than three seconds. Carter yanked open the passenger side door and dived across the seat.

"Head just like that," he hissed. "Don't move. Hands on the wheel." For emphasis, he thumbed the hammer back on the Rommer.

"What's this, you her pimp?" the little man snarled.

The hooker took off. She hadn't seen a thing.

"Start the car, nice and easy."

"Fuck you."

Carter cradled the man's head with his free hand and ground the barrel of the Rommer viciously into his ear.

"All right, all right!" He started the car and eased slowly from the curb.

"Turn right," Carter barked. The man turned. Three blocks farther on, Carter spotted a deep alley. "In here."

He reached over and killed the headlights as they turned. "Stop here!"

They stopped and Carter pocketed the keys. Practically in the same movement he opened the door and shoved the man out. He had barely sprawled, when Carter had him up against the wall, his legs spread.

"Look, I don't know—"

"Shut up."

A fist in the kidneys brought a painful grunt but no more words. A search gave him a fat wallet, a passport, a credentials case, and a Heckler and Koch UP70 automatic pistol.

Inside the credentials case was a badge and an ID card identifying the man as Bruno Lunt, detective inspector, shield G4991411, St. Pauli District, Hamburg.

Carter shook his head in amazement. "What do the police want with me?"

"Routine." The little man shrugged. "Picked you up at the airport. Suspicious acting."

"On whose authority?" Carter asked.

"My own."

"You just lounged around the airport, spotted a suspicious character, and followed me?"

"That's right."

"And what flight was I on?"

"Lufthansa 4113 from Belgrade . . ." He clamped his jaw shut, but it was too late.

Carter gave him another good shot in the kidneys and he went to the ground. The Killmaster put his foot on the back of the man's neck, and ground.

"I'm the police, you fool!" the little man cried.

"I don't give a shit. Someone spotted me getting on the flight in Belgrade and phoned ahead, right?"

No words, but a lot of wriggling. Using his hair, Carter bounced the man's forehead a few times on the bricks, then returned his foot to the back of his neck.

"Right, Bruno?"

"Yes, Jesus, yes . . ."

"Who?"

"I don't know. I never know. I just get a call from Berlin now and then. It's always surveillance. I report, I get an envelope."

Carter thought this over. It was a good guess that little Bruno had already made Otto; von Krumm was far from unknown. But that might not pose a problem if the count moved out fast.

"Get up."

Bruno crawled to his feet. Carter pushed him to the rear of the car and opened the trunk.

"What're you going to do?"

"More important, Bruno, what are *you* going to do?"

Carter took his State Department ID out and waved it in front of the little man's eyes just enough so he could read the official seal and not the name.

"You might not know who those callers are in Berlin, Bruno, but I think you can guess. I'm into something big, bigger than anything you've ever known. The report you're going to file is that you lost me tonight. You got that?"

"*Ja, ja.*"

"If I hear different, and I will hear, I'll have the West German BfV on your ass like flies on shit. You got that?"

"I lost you right outside the airport."

"And my friend?"

"What friend?"

"Good. Stick to shaking down hookers, Bruno. One of those phone calls will put you in a grave someday. Get in the trunk."

The little man scrambled in and Carter shut the lid.

Back at his own car, he waited until von Krumm came by again, and fell in behind the cream-colored Mercedes.

He was big and he was tough, with a muscular build and dark, faintly cruel good looks. He looked as if he could chew nails and stomp any man twice his size for relaxation.

There was something about the man that made you look twice at him, something hard, impressive, and commanding. There was an all-consuming demand in his eyes, the straight, thin, unsmiling line of his mouth, the almost catlike way the muscular six-foot-three-inch form balanced lightly on the balls of his feet.

He leaned tiredly against the wall of the corridor as he pressed the bell of Apartment 6D and then waited. But not even the lines of exhaustion in his face could mask the intensity of his concentrated attention. This was a man who was used to waiting, but at the same time, a man who could spring into action instantly, with no perceptible lag, when action was required.

There were footsteps inside the apartment. A peephole in the door slid aside and a disembodied eye examined the man in the corridor. After a second or so, the peephole snapped shut. Two locks ground noisily and then the door swung open on well-oiled hinges.

A woman stood framed in the doorway. Her age was indeterminate. She could have been anything from twenty-five to forty. Her grooming was perfect. There was no flaw that any man could have found in her makeup. Her figure was a thing of beauty. But like the man in the corridor, her eyes were tired, cynical, and all-knowing. There were no illusions left in her.

"Come in," she said quietly.

She walked from the door, not bothering to close it. He moved in behind her and closed it gently himself.

One shelf of books in a floor-to-ceiling bookcase swung out, and from behind it she took a velvet bag. He joined her at the table as she carefully unwrapped the bag. It opened, and the overhead light danced off a jewel-encrusted watch, two diamond rings, a necklace, and a matching pair of diamond earrings.

The man screwed a jeweler's loupe into his right eye and carefully examined each piece.

"He wants thirty thousand," she said.

"Impossible. I can't move them without completely remounting every piece, and the stones in the rings will have to be recut."

He folded all pieces carefully back into the velvet bag and slipped them into his pocket. Then he took a thick roll of bills from another pocket and counted out twenty thousand American dollars in one pile. He put another twenty one-hundred-dollar bills in a second pile and pushed it across the table to her.

"Your commission."

"Latos called from Marseilles. He's got a big score."

The man shook his head. "Tell him to hold off for a while and take nothing else. I have to be out of the country for a week, perhaps longer."

She moved close enough to press her breasts against his arm. "Can you stay tonight?"

"No," he replied, rising and moving toward the door.

"But it's been so long," she pouted.

"I must leave the day after tomorrow, and there is much to be done."

The door closed behind him before she could argue.

On the street, he paused to light a small cigar. Behind the match and the spiraling smoke, he checked every car, every movement, every window as far as he could see.

Only when his animal instincts told him it was safe to move did he cross the street and get behind the wheel of an ancient Opal.

Two blocks away, a tall, slender figure in black leather sat astride a Triumph motorcycle between two parked trucks. The eyes behind the tinted shield of the helmet watched the Opal pull away.

Only after it had made a turn did the rider start the machine and follow.

Count Otto von Krumm's flat was the penthouse of a seven-story building overlooking the Herbertstrasse, the famous "Street of Harlots."

"It warms me," he said, "to be able to look down at any hour of the day or night and see all that sin."

It was a cheerful apartment, with three guest rooms, a master bedroom suite, a dining room, and living room.

They came into the living room, and Otto dismissed the girl with a kiss on the forehead and a pat on the bottom. When she had gone, he turned to Carter and laughed, as if ashamed of himself.

"What will you drink?"

"Nothing, thanks. You want me coherent, after all."

"Precisely. How do you expect to order your thoughts without a drink? Scotch?"

"Thank you."

"A sober man is a depressing man." Von Krumm walked to the bar and mixed it quickly. Then he produced four bottles with strange shapes and unfamiliar labels. "I'm off scotch, myself. Too dull. Slivovitz with a shot of absinthe. Gets the blood running." He poured and moved back to Carter with the glasses, handing Carter the scotch. "To money and sin."

Carter grinned and drank.

"Now, then," von Krumm said, easing into the plush sofa, "let's have it. I must warn you that my finances are in an excellent state, so whatever you propose must have aesthetic qualities as well as huge financial gain."

"First, is the castle at Bundesdorg suitable for guests?"

"Above the first floor, or the dungeon?" von Krumm chuckled.

"The dungeon, actually. One, maybe two, for at least a week."

"It can be arranged. Will you need a keeper?"

Carter shook his head. "I'll bring my own."

"'Nuf said. Consider it done. What else?"

"Your father's old SS files. I want you to find a Nazi who is dead but could be alive. He must be a man who had access to vast loot and could have fled to South America."

"That shouldn't be any problem. Then what?"

"You become that man."

Von Krumm started. "Oh, dear. He would have to be close to seventy. All that makeup—"

"Otto," Carter interrupted, "let me explain . . ."

For the next hour Carter outlined his plan and what they were going after, leaving out only Vadim Vinnick's name. The more he talked, the more von Krumm became interested. By the time the Killmaster was through, the count was smiling like a cat eating cream, and filling in details of his own.

"Lovely, lovely, Nicholas, a true tour de force! I'll leave for the castle in the morning."

Carter stood. He placed the wallet, credentials case, revolver, and car keys he had taken from the Hamburg cop on the table. Von Krumm leaned forward and flipped open the credentials case.

"The reason for your delay?"

Carter nodded. "He does odd jobs for a Berlin source. It's probably a central number for all the East bloc agencies who want surveillance done but don't have a man of their own in place."

Von Krumm chuckled. "Certainly not in Hamburg. I think the last man they had here fornicated himself to death. What do you need?"

"I think I put the fear of hell in him, but it wouldn't hurt to add an exclamation point to it."

"No problem," Otto said. "I have a couple of friends who can return all this to the gentleman and cause him great distress at the same time. Anything else?"

"Yes. I was going to fly to Amsterdam tonight, but they have another watcher at the airport. If you can get me a clean car I'll drive over. Also, have someone drop my rental at the airport."

Von Krumm grabbed the phone and dialed. It was answered at once. Less than a minute later he hung up and turned to Carter. "Do you know the Hansa Theatre on Steindamm?"

"Yes."

"The doorman's name is Kurt. Trade keys with him. He'll point his car out to you."

Suddenly the blonde, completely naked, appeared in the doorway. "Otto, when do you come to bed?"

"Now, my dear," von Krumm replied, and traded glances with Carter. "Isn't she lovely?"

"A true gem."

"Sure you won't join us?"

"Otto, you have no morals."

The count was laughing as he moved to the bedroom door. "Absolutely none, my friend. Absolutely none!"

SEVEN

At noon Carter descended to the lobby. The desk
clerk caught his eye and beckoned him over. It was a
message from Lorena: *Room 712, the Americain*.

Carter went to a phone booth, called the hotel, and
asked for room 712.

"Yes?"

"How about lunch?"

"Sounds marvelous," she replied.

"The Papeneiland is near you."

"Twenty minutes," she said breathlessly, and hung
up.

Carter dialed a second number and waited several
rings before it was answered. There was no vocal response from the other end of the line, just silence.

"I would like to speak to Mortimer, please."

"Who wants him?" came the gravelly reply.

"Nick."

"A minute."

It was almost five before the familiar voice came on the line. "Mr. Carter, is it?"

"It is, Mortimer. How goes it?"

"The usual aches and pains but I manage to get around. What can I do fer ya?"

"I have a job. It starts here and goes over the frontier. Probably take a couple of weeks. Want to talk about it?"

"Love to. Business has been terrible, it has, what with this AIDS problem. All me girls are thinkin' of becomin' secretaries, they are."

"At the place around six. Be dark by then."

"That'll be dandy, Mr. Carter. We'll have us a pint."

"Cheers, mate," Carter said, and hung up.

He walked to the main canal and turned up Prinsengracht to number Two. He passed the tunnel entrance to the café's cellar that once led under the canal and was used by seventeenth-century Catholics as a secret way of getting together for worship. The Papeneiland claimed to be the oldest café in Amsterdam, tracing its history back to its first coffin-maker owner who served drinks on the side when business was slow.

"One, sir?"

"Two, for lunch," Carter replied.

He was shown to a table in the depths that needed the candle on the wall to read the menu.

Lorena appeared right on time, looking a bit frumpy in a scarf, a loose-fitting tweed coat, and knee-high boots.

"Welcome to Amsterdam," she said, brushing his lips with her own and taking the opposite chair.

"I'm having beer."

"Fine," she said with a nod.

The waiter brought a second beer and two newspaper-sized menus. Lorena waited until he was gone before she spoke.

"Thank you for taking this on."

"I didn't have much choice. A very hard lady named Ilse let me know that if I didn't, she was going to make a corpse out of me."

"Ilse tends to exaggerate."

"Oh?" Carter said. "How well do you know her?"

"Not very well, but she is devoted to my brother."

"I know. And I don't think she was exaggerating."

"You're mad at me."

"A little," Carter admitted, "but I'll get over it. The stakes are too high not to."

"How does he look?"

Carter decided to be blunt. "Like any dying man with the wolves nipping at his heels."

Lorena took it without blinking. "You had problems?"

Carter told her the whole story. At the part about burying the woman in the snow he thought she might crack, but she held up.

"Then the situation is much worse. He has many enemies in the agencies of the other Eastern bloc countries."

"That's his problem," Carter said. "Mine is satisfying his demands and getting that list. What about Fabian Huzel?"

"I've been following him for the last three days. He is as wily as a fox. He has a house in the Boorstadt district west of the city. Also two flats. One is in Dijkstraat, off the New Market. The other is on Amstrel on the canal. He never stays in the same place two nights in a row. He also has four cars scattered around the city. He constantly changes them."

"A very cautious man."

"Very. The house and both flats are like fortresses. He even keeps dogs in all of them. I managed to get close to him twice on the street. He's armed at all times, a pistol under his coat in the back and another in an ankle holster. And I'd say from the looks of him he can use them."

"What about business?"

"Legitimately, he's a member of the Diamond Exchange, but he's rarely there. He also has a small shop on Potterstraat where he buys and sells... legally. It probably makes a pittance compared to his fencing. The shop is run by one of his mistresses."

"One?" Carter replied, cocking an eyebrow. "How many does he have?"

Lorena smiled. "Four, besides the one in the shop. He's like a pimp, only they don't sell their bodies. They are contacted by thieves all over Europe and the Middle East when the thieves make a score."

"Huzel picks up and pays off through his mistresses?"

She nodded. "Huzel himself never actually meets the thief. The police can't touch him."

"Not an easy man to pin down," Carter murmured. "But there must be a way. In the meantime, let's eat."

They ordered *hutspot*, a steaming beef stew with kale, potatoes, and sausage, all of it washed down with excellent beer. Over coffee they resumed the discussion.

"How about routine?"

"The women contact Huzel if they have anything. He picks all of his messages up from a service."

"My God, Lorena," Carter growled, "you're making this as difficult as hell. From what you've told me, there is no way of figuring any one place he might be."

She leaned forward, her voice scarcely a whisper. "There is one thing. It's a little bit of a long shot, but . . ."

"What is it?"

"He's flying out tomorrow morning. The first leg is to Paris, but I did a little bribing and found out that he's bouncing from plane to plane. The last leg is from Lisbon to Buenos Aires."

Carter's eyes narrowed. "That means he's on his way to meet our pigeon. Doesn't leave much time . . ."

"Nick, I think I've found two weaknesses, maybe the only ones he has, and they could put him into the open. Huzel is deathly afraid to fly."

"So?" Carter said, listening with only half an ear now, his mind racing, trying to pick apart what Lorena had already told him.

"As I said, it's a long shot, but . . . well, the other weakness is his mother."

"Lorena . . ."

"Let me finish. His mother's ashes are interred in a tomb in Christ's Church. That's in Ijmuiden, about ten miles west of Amsterdam. I hit on it when I was going over the file my brother sent me on Huzel."

"I went over that file," Carter said. "Wait a minute. I remember now. He visits that tomb every Sunday afternoon. But what good will that do us? Tomorrow is Friday."

"I was out there, Nick. I had a cup of tea with the caretaker, told him I was a writer doing a story on cemeteries. I got the conversation around to people who regularly tend the graves. Huzel comes so often that the caretaker remembers him. Nick, he remembers several other times—other than Sundays—when Huzel came out to the grave."

Carter's eyes were wide. "You mean he's so afraid of flying that he goes out and talks to Momma before he takes off?"

Lorena nodded. "The dates match with the travel record we have in his file for the last six months. It's a long shot, but . . ."

"But it's better than nothing," Carter said, dropping some bills on the table. "I'll call you at your hotel."

Lorena grasped him by the elbow. "Why don't you just come by?"

"A lot to do, but I'll try." He gave her a quick kiss on the cheek as they parted in front of the restaurant.

He took a water taxi on the canals as far as he could go toward the western part of the city. He got off at Leidsestraat, the wide boulevard that led to the highway into the west country. He found a cab idling at the curb when he climbed the stone steps from the water's edge to the street.

"Ijmuiden, Christ's Church cemetery."

Twenty minutes later he gave the driver some bills to wait, and walked the old cemetery until he found the Huzel tomb. Then he walked the perimeter, checking out every tree and finding the caretaker's shack.

Basically the area was level, but there was a rise about forty yards from the entrance to the tomb. There were a few trees and two large grave markers that could be used for concealment.

It would have to be done from there. Anywhere on

the road itself or the approaches to the tomb would be too open.

He returned to the taxi and had the driver troll the streets of the village until he spotted a long-term parking lot beside a grocery co-op. One look told him that it was also used as a commuter lot for the bus stop into Amsterdam. The coin machines would belch out tickets for up to a week's duration.

"Where to now?" the driver asked.

"Back to the city," Carter replied, checking his watch. "Just drop me a little east of the Damrak."

The driver's eyebrows shot up a bit, but he flipped his windshield wipers back on and slipped the taxi into gear.

Carter could almost read the man's thoughts. There was no way a local could figure out a foreigner's tastes. The well-dressed gentleman had visited a fine old cemetery, and then wants to be taken to the red-light district!

The seat of sex in Amsterdam is not as loud or as garish as the Reeperbahn of Hamburg, but it is just as varied and every bit as alive.

Twice Carter almost got lost. The little shows that advertised sex aids, live sex, peep shows, and the eerily crimson-lighted windows with scarcely dressed women were so much alike that it was difficult to find a landmark.

At last he spotted the sign and turned into the Yum-Yum Club. A king's ransom in guilders got him by the bored matron at the door. Through dingy velvet curtains he stepped into the dimly lit main room of the club.

The show was on. On a slightly elevated stage, a young man and a not-so-young woman were locked in anything but love. It was all carnal to the soft accompaniment of flutes and violins.

"You like a table down front? Good to see all the action." He was shorter than Carter but twice as wide, Chinese, and looked a little like a young Mao Ze-Dong with muscles.

"No, the bar will be fine," Carter replied. "I have business with Mr. Potts. Tell him that Nick is here."

"I will do that."

Carter was halfway through a stein of beer when the Chinese returned.

"This way, please."

Carter was led up a flight of stairs, down a corridor, and up to a door marked Office. He could easily have found the way himself, but the Chinese looked like a man who liked to do his duty.

Carter rapped on the door and a voice like velvet said, "Enter."

The office was like day compared to the club below's night. It was a pleasant air-conditioned room that offered Oriental rugs, a mahogany reading table with an assortment of newspapers and magazines, all in Dutch, a mahogany settee, and, in the corner and protected by a desk, an almond-eyed girl with porcelain-smooth off-white skin and straight black hair. She wore a bright print dress and an exotic silver necklace, and she finished a line of typing before she glanced up.

"You are Mr. Carter?"

"I am."

Apparently there was no intercom because she rose, smoothed her skirt, knocked at a dark-stained door. She opened it and, coming up on one foot and showing nice legs, stuck her head around the edge.

Carter didn't hear what was said, but the result was satisfactory. Pivoting on the same leg she came to rest, the door swinging wide and her balance regained. Her smile and shy nod were his invitation to enter.

He smiled his way past her and entered hell.

Mortimer Potts's inner sanctum was chaos, litter and rubbish piled floor-to-ceiling across the whole room. A huge desk sat in the middle of it all, and behind the desk, Mortimer Potts.

He was a little, thin man, poorly dressed in a baggy suit, a soiled shirt, and a frayed red tie. A few wisps of stringy hair flapped about on top of his head like remnants dropped from someone else's comb.

"Mr. Carter, gar, it's good to see ya again!" He stood, extending his hand, and Carter moved forward to shake it.

It was his smile that made Mortimer Potts lovable. His lips were thin like his wrinkled face, but when they parted, revealing a dentist's nightmare, his grin lit up the world.

"Mortimer, you haven't changed a bit. Haven't seen you in a year or more and I swear it's the same suit."

"'Course it is! Gar, I buy a new suit and the tax people'll say I'm makin' money, they will!" He swept old magazines, newspapers, and a few mouse droppings off a chair. "Have a seat, lad. Jolly good of you to bring some business me way, Mr. Carter. Times has been bad."

Carter sat. "How's Miriam?"

"Died, she did. Three months ago, poor thing."

"Three months ago? And you haven't remarried yet?" Mortimer had a way of picking wealthy, fat, shrewish wives, but he always seemed to outlive them.

To Carter's knowledge, the dearly departed Miriam had been number six.

"Ah, I think them days is over fer ol' Mortimer. I just ain't young like I used ta be." He rubbed his hands together and flashed another wide grin. "But enough of me sorry troubles. What will ya be into this time?"

"First," Carter said, "can you be away for a couple of weeks?"

"Oh, lord, yes. Got me that Chinee brother and sister. They run the place now, really. And honest? They account fer every penny. What's up?"

Carter told him on a need-to-know basis.

"An' ya want me to stay with him in this bloody castle?" Potts exclaimed when Carter had finished. "Why not just kill the bugger?"

"Can't do that. I may need information out of him along the way. I'll set up communications from wherever I am to you, and you get out of him what I need."

"Ah, an' ya know I'm good at that," Potts cackled. "When do ya want to snatch him?"

Carter stood and began pacing, ignoring the debris in his path. "That's the problem. We've only got about fifteen hours."

"Ah, dear me. What are we gonna need?"

"An ambulance, or a closed-in vehicle with red crosses that could be mistaken for one. It should look like it comes from a private hospital."

"Go on," Potts replied, scratching on a pad.

"A motorbike, old, something we can just dump in a canal. Three uniforms, a driver, nurse, and intern. Some medical papers showing he has a rare disease . . ."

"Terminal?" Potts asked, glancing up from his notes.

"No, but life-threatening would be good."

"No problem. Go on. Passports?"

"I should think we can use our own," Carter replied, "but you might add medical identification."

"Very well. How will you take him?"

"That's the sticky part," Carter sighed. "He's a very nasty character, has a reputation of shooting people when they get too near him. I'll need an air gun, powerful and accurate."

"A pellet?"

"Or dart. We don't want to have to perform any surgery to get the pellet out."

"That, of course, will be the hardest part, but I think I can do it. Where are you stayin'?"

Carter almost gave him his own hotel, then remembered. "The Americain, room Seven-twelve. Don't use my name, just ask for the room."

"The nurse?"

"Yes."

Potts stood. "I've got a lot to do. I'll call as soon as it's done."

At the Americain, Carter climbed the service stairs to the tenth floor, then walked down to the seventh.

"Yes?" came a whisper in response to his knock.

"It's me."

The door was opened at once and he slid inside.

"I ordered a tray of sandwiches and some beer."

Carter kissed her lightly and slipped out of his coat. They sat side by side on the sofa and ate.

"You went to the cemetery?"

"Yes. It's not perfect, but it will do. Do you think that old caretaker would think it odd if you showed up for coffee in the morning?"

"No, I doubt it. Why?"

Carter dropped a small vial in her lap. "Two of those in his coffee. He'll go out like a light and stay out for about three hours. Chances are when he wakes up he'll think he just made a boor of himself and fell asleep on you."

"Good. What then?"

He explained the whole plan to her, and where they would be taking Huzel once they had him.

"Can we trust this Mortimer chap?"

Carter nodded. "Honor among thieves. If Huzel wanted to put the snatch on me, Mortimer would be more than happy to oblige. But since it's the other way around and I'm paying him first, he'll see it through to the end, guaranteed."

He finished the rest of his sandwich and sat back to light a cigarette.

"How do we work it once we get to Argentina?" Lorena asked, clearing away the tray and settling in beside him.

"I have another friend. His name is Otto von Krumm. You'll go in with him as his daughter. Otto will be posing as an ex-Nazi. The two of you will put the fear of God into Glaskov. Hopefully, between you, Otto, and myself, we'll have him so confused he won't know what to do."

"I don't understand . . ."

"You will. I'll go through the whole thing with you tomorrow night at the castle. In the meantime, come here."

"I thought you'd never ask," she said with a laugh, and slid across the sofa into his arms.

She put her arms around him, and her warm, firm

breasts, her long thighs, her lips, and her belly all seemed to press against him at once. When he touched her he felt her quiver like a thoroughbred. They clasped each other furiously in a tangle of arms, legs, hands, and lips. She lay back on the sofa and let him take her with her head hanging over the edge and one foot on the floor, like a schoolgirl furtively making love in her parents' house.

When they finally came back to their senses, she laughed at the sight of her torn skirt, her panties crumpled into a ball on the floor, her unfastened bra and her sweater pulled up around her neck.

"Shall we go into the bedroom and act like adults this time?" she asked, grinning.

"Not nearly as much fun," he chuckled.

Then the phone rang. She answered it and handed it to Carter.

"Hello?"

"Got everything, Mr. Carter. Right down to the little dart all dipped and ready."

"Good work, Mortimer. Pick up the nurse in front of the Americain at six in the morning. Where's the motorbike?"

"In the alley behind the club. Key's on a string in the gas tank."

"See you then." Carter hung up. He turned to Lorena. "I'll go out very early and make sure the two back gates of the place are sealed off so we get no unwanted mourners from that end. When you get there with Mortimer, go straight to the caretaker's cottage and make sure he's taken care of."

She nodded her understanding and Carter stood, and then frowned when she saw him righting his clothes.

EIGHT

It was still dark when Carter checked out with his small flight bag and took a taxi to the Yum-Yum Club. In the rear of the club he found the motorbike, a big BMW.

One light rap on the door of the club and it was opened by the bulky Chinese. Wordlessly, Carter was handed a set of leathers and a helmet. He changed right there in the tiny hallway and stuffed his clothes in the bag. As he was leaving, he traded the bag for a long, leather-covered case. This he strapped to the BMW and kicked it into life.

Minutes later he was in the western part of the city fighting a slight drizzle and heavy fog. The fog, he thought, would be both good and bad. Hopefully it wouldn't deter Huzel from talking to his Momma.

In Ijmuiden, he located the long-term parking lot and fed coins into the meter until he had enough slips for a week's parking. Back on the bike to the cemetery and church.

Everything was quiet and there was no light on in the caretaker's cottage. He went directly to the spot he had picked out, and hid the case containing the air rifle and the case among the stones. Then he jogged around the perimeter to the two rear entrances. As quietly as possible, he closed the gates and hung the No Admittance signs on both of them.

The fog was still heavy but the gray light of dawn was valiantly trying to penetrate it as he rode back to the village of Ijmuiden. He located a small roadside café and sat at a front table by the window and had breakfast.

He was on a second cup of coffee when he spotted the ambulance go past. His watch said a little after nine o'clock.

He paid for the breakfast and rode the bike back to the cemetery. At the main entrance he saw no sign of the ambulance, but Mortimer, in a pair of blue coveralls and a heavy jacket, was moving litter around with a rake.

Carter rode on through the cemetery to the caretaker's cottage and honked twice. The door opened and Lorena's head popped out.

"Done," she murmured.

Carter nodded and wheeled the BMW around to a lean-to in the rear of the cottage. He killed the engine and jogged through the stones to his place of concealment.

When he had the air rifle out of its case and assembled, he lifted one of the two darts that Mortimer had supplied and pulled off the plastic cap over the point. Then he crimped the fine plastic flanges and slid it into the firing chamber. Next came the CO_2 cartridge. When its head was pierced, he heard the slight whoosh of air release that would fire the dart. Carefully, he removed the second dart's tip and set it on the gravestone beside him. With the scope sight and the short range, he was sure he wouldn't need it, but it was there just in case.

Then, resisting the desire for a cigarette, Carter wormed his way down between the stones to wait.

The moment he heard the car the Killmaster became instantly alert. Through the stones he could see the Opal moving through the fog. It turned into the gate, passing Mortimer without slowing. About thirty feet from the tomb the Opal stopped and Huzel got out.

He was a handsome devil, Carter thought, if you liked them mean. He would be a great success with ladies who preferred their sex swift and brutal.

Huzel paused beside the car, his eyes taking in every tree and stone. He took a cigarette from a black case and lit it.

The man, Carter thought, was like an animal, always wary, alert, sniffing the air for danger.

At last Huzel was apparently satisfied. He moved forward.

Carter's eyes drifted from Huzel to Mortimer. He had abandoned his rake and was closing the gate. He hung the No Admittance sign and was gone. With the fog it was doubtful that they would have any more visitors, but the closed gate would provide some insurance.

Huzel was almost to the tomb now, a ring of keys in his hand. When he reached the iron gate of the tomb's door, he stopped and slipped one of the keys into the lock.

Carter put the man's neck in the cross hairs of the

sight. He wasn't moving. It was the simplest shot in the world.

He squeezed the trigger.

The little dart entered the side of Huzel's neck and hung there like an enlarged bee sting.

The carotid is the principal artery of the neck; it is as thick as a garden hose. As Huzel felt the sting he jerked his head back. His hand moved toward the holster, and his heart pumped with dispassionate efficiency. Arteries carry blood from the heart to the tissues. This one went straight—that critically short distance—to his brain.

The Killmaster was reaching for the second dart, when Huzel pitched forward. He had barely hit the ground when Carter whistled.

Everything had been coordinated.

Lorena sprinted from the caretaker's cottage. She opened the front gate just as Mortimer, in the ambulance, drove out of the trees. Lorena didn't pause but ran right to the back gates and opened them.

Carter methodically went through Huzel's pockets, transferring everything he found to his own.

"One shot?" Mortimer asked.

"That's all it took," Carter grunted.

Together they hefted Huzel to the rear. When the doors were open they sat him up and undressed him. When he was dressed again in a hospital gown and a heavy terry-cloth robe, he was strapped onto the gurney and covered.

Lorena appeared at the rear of the ambulance. "Caretaker's still out, no cars on the road."

Carter produced the two rings of keys he had taken from Huzel's pockets. The larger ring held the keys to his flats and house and probably his shop. Keys on the smaller ring belonged to the fleet of cars he used.

Carter passed the car-ring to Lorena along with the parking lot stamps, and then turned to Mortimer. The man had already peeled off the windbreaker, flannel shirt, and coveralls. Beneath them he wore the white smock and pants of a driver or orderly.

"Drive to the café behind the church and have coffee," Carter instructed. "Lorena, as soon as you leave Huzel's car in the parking lot, head for the ambulance."

They both nodded.

"Now," Carter said, "where do we rendezvous?"

"At Weesp, in the parking lot of the school," Lorena answered.

"Good enough," Carter said. "Let's move!"

Mortimer headed back toward the village first. Two minutes later, Lorena followed in Huzel's car. Two minutes after that, Carter fired up the motorcycle and headed for Amsterdam.

Carter felt a clammy sweat roll down his back as he parked the bike and slung the courier's bag over his shoulder. It was just past noon. He had already gone through Huzel's country house and one of the two flats in the city. He hadn't found what he was looking for in either place.

Did Huzel keep the records of his foreign customers in his head? Did he memorize every address, contact method, the telephone number of everyone he bought and sold from?

Carter hoped to strike pay dirt here, in the second flat.

The houses were all in a row, exactly alike, stretching from one canal to another. He located the number and entered the hall. Cooking smells assailed his nostrils and somewhere a radio played jazz.

He took the steps to the third floor two at a time and attacked the lock. The fifth key on the ring opened the door.

The drapes were closed. Carter found the light switch by feel and flipped it. He was in a rectangular room with windows on both sides. Scatter rugs partially covered the bare wood floors.

He lifted each of the rugs. No safe.

There was a cluttered desk in one corner. It took him five minutes to go through the papers on top and rifle the drawers. He found nothing that would help him down the road.

The bedroom was nearly square in shape, with an alcove that held a stall shower but no tub. A double bed with no footboard stood against one wall, a mahogany highboy against another. A small mirrored vanity occupied part of the third wall. Above the vanity mirror was another, square mirror, slightly recessed into the wall.

Carter went through every drawer and lifted the paintings on the walls.

Nothing.

The kitchen, which was entered through the second living room door, was just a kitchen, rather long but narrow, and had no outside door. The sink was yellow-stained and chipped, with an open space and a garbage pail below, and cabinets above. The stove was a three-burner with a small removable oven; the refrigerator was ancient-looking and noisy.

Back in the living room office, Carter lit a cigarette and made his mind work. It was possible that Huzel kept his illegal records in the safe of his legal shop in the old town.

Possible, Carter thought, but not probable.

If the man was so wary about everything else, he would be especially paranoid about anything on paper that might send him to jail.

And the jewels.

The illegal jewels he was fencing had to be somewhere. Lorena had said that Huzel had made five pickups in the time she had followed him. He would not have had the time to resell those pickups.

Carter wandered back into the bedroom.

Then it hit him. The mirrored vanity. Why a *second* mirror, and why was it recessed into the wall?

He used a nail file from the vanity on the crack around the mirror. Near the bottom right-hand corner, he hit an obstacle. He heard a click as he pushed harder, and the mirror swung outward.

Carefully, he inspected the safe.

He found the maker's name, and closed his eyes for a moment while he dusted off the files of his memory. He recalled the system and it took his trained fingertips fifteen minutes to find the combination.

The opening wasn't large but the safe was deep and the whole of the back was filled with neat packets of currency bound together with paper strips. And if the new one-hundred-dollar bill on the top of the brick Carter lifted out was an indicator, he estimated that, give or take a few grand, he was looking at fifty thousand dollars.

That figured, Carter mused. Huzel was in a cash business.

Underneath the bills, he found a tray of diamonds

and two velvet bags of miscellaneous jewels.

Now the safe was empty and he had still struck out.

Then he remembered the manufacturer and a particular added attraction to this model.

Five minutes later he located the pull release that opened a panel in the back of the safe. In the indentation behind the panel was a flat logbook. One glance and Carter knew he had what he wanted. It was all in coded symbols, but easy to decipher if the person doing it knew Huzel's business.

The jewels and cash he put in a pillowcase. It and the book went into his courier bag. He closed the safe, made sure everything was in place, and moved quickly back to the street.

He rode to the Yum-Yum Club and entered through the rear door. The beautiful Oriental girl was in her office on the second floor. Carter dropped the pillowcase on the desk.

"Put this away for Mr. Potts. He'll be back in a week or so."

Back on the bike, he wound his way through late-afternoon traffic to the southern edge of the city. Fifteen minutes later he was coasting through the small village of Weesp. He was just past the old school when the ambulance pulled from the parking lot and fell in behind him.

A mile outside the village he turned left into a narrow tractor lane. Two hundred yards in front of him he could see the Amstel River.

He speeded up and pulled his feet up until he was standing on the seat in a semi-crouch.

Ten feet from the riverbank he jumped straight into the air.

The bike sailed out over the river for several feet before it fell into the water and sank out of sight.

Carter came to earth and rolled to his feet. Lorena had the rear door of the ambulance open. He piled in and at once began peeling off the leathers.

"You found it?" she asked.

Carter nodded. "Yeah. Mortimer?"

"Eh?"

"I've just made you a moderately wealthy man."

"Music to me ears," the man chuckled, and moved the van back toward the highway.

The road switchbacked for about eight miles and then the lights of the frontier posts gleamed through the fog. A long straight street led directly to the Dutch side. Potts dimmed his headlights and joined the line of vehicles waiting to be processed.

The Dutch border guard barely glanced at Potts and waved them through perfunctorily.

It was a different story a hundred yards farther on at the German gate.

A stern-looking border guard poked his head through the window. "Papers."

Potts handed over the medical papers and their passports. The guard carried the documents to a lighted window where a colleague sat.

"Don't sweat it if they check us," Mortimer murmured. "Dope flows like the river Nile the other way into the Netherlands and Amsterdam, but from Amsterdam into Germany it's another story."

He was right. A minute later they were bundled out

of the ambulance and it was searched. They and the medical bags were searched.

"You are the doctor?"

"Yes," Carter replied.

The guard gestured toward Huzel's blanket-covered form on the gurney. "What is wrong with him?"

"A severe case of hydroxia pormangalia."

"Eh?" the man said, taking a slight step backward. "Is that a communicable disease?"

"Not at all," Carter replied. "He needs rest and constant supervision. We are taking him to the clinic in Essen."

"Ah."

The papers were handed back to Potts, the gate was lifted, and they were waved through.

On the other side, Lorena tapped Carter's shoulder. "What is hydroxia pormangalia?"

"Damned if I know," Carter chuckled.

There was no speed limit on the German side even though they were traveling a secondary road and not on the autobahn. In spite of the slippery road conditions, car after car, usually German, sped past them. Carter shook his head. He was forced by circumstances to take so many chances, he couldn't understand anyone taking risks who didn't need to.

The German department of highways had apparently never heard of rock salt or didn't believe in using it. Although the roads were plowed, only the top layer of snow was off, and the surface was covered with a thick, rutty layer of ice and hard-packed snow.

"Bloody idiots," Potts groused as a big Mercedes

flew by them, fishtailing, the driver nearly losing it.

"It's getting close," Carter said. "Not much over a mile."

It was exactly a mile. Carter pointed and Potts spun the wheel.

"My God," Lorena exclaimed, her eyes peering upward through the windshield. "It looks like a Gothic movie set!"

Carter chuckled. "It does at that, doesn't it."

Potts wasn't happy. "I got to stay there? The place is probably bloody haunted."

Otto Krumm opened the massive oak door just as Carter stepped from the rear of the ambulance with Lorena close behind him.

But it was a new Otto. His hair was silver and his face was perfectly aged, with sunken eyes and wrinkles over wrinkles. Even his posture was different, his usually erect body seeming to be shrunken inside his clothes. The voice when he spoke was wheezy, asthmatic.

"What do you think?"

"Fantastic," Carter replied, nodding his appreciation of the total make-over.

Von Krumm put out his hand. "So glad you had a safe trip, Herr Huzel. Allow me to introduce myself. SS General Erwin Bittrich. I thought it best that I outrank the alias of our prey."

Carter smiled. "A wise decision, General." He nodded to Lorena. "Your daughter."

Von Krumm turned to the woman and extended his arms. "Magda, my darling," he cackled, "it's so good to see you again after all these years!"

"When yer bloody family reunion is over," Mortimer Potts said from the rear of the ambulance, "how about a hand with this garbage?"

When Huzel was established in the dungeon room that had been prepared for him, the four of them returned to a small study on the first floor.

Von Krumm explained the arrangement to Potts. "He has everything he needs down there. You can feed him via the dumbwaiter, and communicate with him on the intercom."

"He never has to see my face, then?" Potts asked.

"Never. There are three phones in the house, two in the upstairs bedrooms, one here. Nick can reach you direct if he has need of more information."

"I can also use you as a dummy," Carter added, "if I have to make Glaskov think I'm getting prices."

Potts frowned. "How do I get the bloke to talk?"

"Easy," Carter replied. "Give him a choice . . . talk or starve. I go up to Frankfurt and fly out tomorrow. You two follow on the day after. Otto, can you have papers ready for Lorena by then?"

The count shrugged. "No problem. We'll be traveling with Swiss passports, a professor of law and his daughter."

Carter stood, tapping the book he had taken from Huzel's safe. "Now if you'll excuse me, I've got a lot of deciphering and memorizing to do."

He left the room. Mortimer returned to the ambulance to fetch their bags. Von Krumm turned to Lorena and put his hand on her knee.

"You are remarkably beautiful, a very sensuous woman, my dear. I'm looking forward to the next week.

I am sure we shall get along fine." His voice no longer creaked with age.

Lorena lifted his hand and placed it on his own knee. "I'm sure we will, Count von Krumm, if we both remember who we are . . . Daddy."

NINE

The flight was long and boring, a Lufthansa out of Frankfurt nonstop to Rio. He'd seen the movie twice before on other flights, the food, even in first class, still tasted like half-cooked plastic, and the foghornlike snoring of the passenger seated behind him kept Carter from getting much-needed sleep. Even the attentions of the comely and well-endowed flight attendant did little to ease the boredom. The 5:30 A.M. landing came none too soon.

Customs gave him no trouble with the Fabian Huzel passport, and less than an hour after landing he was in a suite at the Leme Palace.

He direct-dialed the Rio office of Amalgamated Press and Wire Services, Buck Waters's private number. He let it ring three times and hung up. He dialed again, let it ring once, and hung up again.

Then he dialed the switchboard operator. "I'd like to

send a telegram, please, and charge it to my room."

"Go ahead, senhor."

"Senhor Enrique Bolivar, Rancho Corinto, Paranavi. Have arrived Rio. Await your instructions transportation. Suite Eleven-ten, Leme Palace, Huzel. That's it."

The girl read it back. "Will there be anything else?"

"Not for the moment. Thank you."

Carter took the elevator to the basement and the exercise, steam room, and pool.

"Just towels and a locker, please," he said to the attendant.

"No massage, senhor?"

"No."

He undressed at the locker and showered before doing a few laps in the pool. Then he tied a towel around his waist and entered the steam room. Two men were already on the benches, a fat, wheezing businessman, and Buck Waters.

Carter climbed to the top bench, settled back with his eyes closed, and let the soothing steam envelop him. Fifteen minutes later the fat man left and Waters slid down the bench until he was right beside Carter. He took a Beretta automatic from between his legs and passed it to the Killmaster.

"What else do you need?"

"Put out the word that an old SS general named Erwin Bittrich is heading this way to contact his Odessa pals."

Waters chuckled. "What's left of the Odessa is a bunch of old, old men who could care less anymore. After Mengele went, the rest of them gave up. The Fourth Reich is dead, Nick."

"I know that and you know that, but some people might still get antsy."

"Is someone really coming?"

Carter nodded. "Traveling Swiss under the names Otto and Magda Goldolph. The Mossad got anybody down here left as bait?"

"Yeah, a couple. I do a little checking now and then for them, but they haven't turned any stones over for a while."

"No matter," Carter said. "Put Otto in touch with them. He'll take the ball from there. And let it be known that he's looking for an old traitor, a Gruppen-führer named Graf von Wassner."

"Will do. Then what?"

"Get Otto four good men, all locals and armed to the teeth. He'll take it from there."

"Anything official on this?"

"Nothing on paper."

"Jesus, Nick, the crap you come up with."

"Nature of the beast," Carter replied, rising. "I've been in a steel cocoon all night. Gonna get a few hours' sleep, then lay down a bit of a smoke screen."

"You want some company?" Waters asked.

"Not yours," Carter said with a grin. "Got a hunch I'll have someone on my heels from the other side until I leave Rio."

Back in the suite, he stripped and passed out.

It was just after two in the afternoon when Carter's mental alarm went off. He called room service and ordered coffee. He showered and shaved while he was waiting for it, then stretched out on the bed to drink it.

He was getting dressed when the phone rang. "Yes?"

"There is an envelope in your box, Senhor Huzel. It came by messenger."

"Thank you."

Ten minutes later he checked at the desk. There were two envelopes. His name was scrawled across both of them, but in different hands. He ripped open the first one, and smiled.

Welcome to Brazil, Herr Huzel, the note said in fancy typed script. *A car will pick you up at your hotel at nine sharp tomorrow morning. Bolivar.*

The note in the second envelope made the hair on the back of Carter's neck stand up: *Huzel: I am in Room 419. Give me a call this evening. Perhaps we could have dinner and conversation. Verna Rashkin.*

The note brought home to Carter the one chance they were taking. The two people he would be bidding against for the jewels were Ravel Bourlein from Paris, and Verna Rashkin from New York.

Vadim Vinnick's words came back to him: "It is highly unlikely that such adversaries have ever met face-to-face. All three of them make an effort to keep a low profile. But it is possible. If that happens, you must be prepared to change the plan midstream."

Carter slipped the envelopes into his pocket as he entered the bar.

He would liked to have broached the problem after he had arrived at Rancho Corinto.

The hotel bar was about half full. He took one of the stools and ordered a vodka and orange juice. He sipped it slowly, watching and listening to the others in the bar. They were mostly couples, but there were a few solo men, sitting alone as he was. Nobody seemed to be paying any undue interest in him.

He had a second drink and went into the dining room. He had scarcely ordered when he was pretty sure he spotted Bolivar's man.

He was dark and young, too young to be hanging around the lobby of the Leme. His manner and his suit didn't indicate that kind of money. It was also the dark, watchful eyes. They were trying not to dart Carter's way, but they did. And each time, the Killmaster picked up on it.

Carter stretched lunch and lounged over coffee. By the time he paid the check and walked through the lobby, he knew he would have a tail. The dark young man was literally dancing to be after him.

Outside, Carter crawled into the first cab in the line. There were two names in Huzel's book with his Rio code, Roberto Perrez and Delgado Raffini. Huzel hadn't done business with either of them for over two years, but that wouldn't matter.

Carter gave the driver the address of Roberto Perrez.

Halfway down the block, he took a quick squint out the rear window. He saw the young man dart from the front door of the hotel and slide into a waiting sedan. The driver had the car moving before the passenger door was closed.

It was a working-class neighborhood filled with apartment buildings, all dingy and looking alike. Carter had the driver wait and went looking. There was a Perrez on the third floor of one building. He walked up some stairs and rang the bell. After a moment the apartment door opened and an old woman looked out.

"I'm looking for Roberto Perrez," Carter said. "Does he live here?"

"He used to live here," she said. She had a slight accent.

"I wonder if you could tell me where I could find him? Are you his mother?"

"I was his mother."

"I don't understand. Aren't you still his mother?"

"My son is dead, senhor... almost seven months now."

"Seven months?"

"How you know my son?"

"I did some business with him," Carter replied.

Her face suddenly became very hard. "Then you are a thief like my son. That's how he die, stealing."

She started to slam the door. Carter held it. "I'm sorry, Senhora Perrez, I didn't know."

"Go away."

Carter fluttered two one-hundred-dollar bills in her face. "The fact is, I owed your son some money. Since he's gone, you might as well have it."

She studied Carter's face, then snatched the money. The door slammed and he returned to the cab. The taxi was waiting. So was the sedan, a half block away. Carter gave the driver the next address and settled back in the seat.

One look told him that the passenger in the sedan was writing down the address Carter had just left.

He wasn't so lucky with Delgado Raffini. The Raffinis had moved and no one seemed to know where they had gone. They weren't listed in any phone directory, but then the poor or the underworld of Rio were probably never listed. Also, the neighbors took him for police and would say nothing.

More for show than anything else, Carter tried the

local stores. It was a druggist who, for a twenty dropped on the counter, came up with an address. He thought that Senhora Raffini had returned to his store to fill a prescription some time after she had moved. He dug around in a drawer until he found it, and gave Carter an address several blocks down the same street.

It was also an old, run-down building. Carter walked up to the third floor and knocked.

The door was opened by a small, dark-haired woman in her early thirties. She must have been very pretty once, but now she looked gaunt and tired.

"Senhora Raffini?"

"*Sim.*"

"I'd like to talk to your husband, Delgado. Is he home?"

"Who you, police?"

"No. I've done some good business with your husband in the past. I haven't heard from him for a while."

She threw back her head and laughed. "And you won't for a long while. The asshole is in prison!" Suddenly she pulled open the loose robe she wore. She was wearing nothing beneath it. "But you can do a little business with me!"

Carter pressed a hundred into her hand. "You tell Delgado when he gets out that Amsterdam is still buying."

He left her with her mouth—and robe—still open, and returned to the cab.

"Where to now, back to hotel?"

"Not quite yet," Carter replied. "Just drive around for a couple of hours. Show me the city and a couple of nice bars with naked women."

Carter leaned back in the seat and smiled as he lit a cigarette.

Bolivar's little boy would report back that Herr Huzel was his usual self . . . always doing business.

Carter gave the two in the sedan fits for another two hours. He stopped at several bars, establishing a routine each time. The driver would wait in front; Carter would enter, order a drink at the bar, watch one of the strippers gyrate a little, then return to the taxi and move on.

Each time, one of the two in the sedan—the young one or his partner, a cut-down version of King Kong with a Pancho Villa mustache—would check Carter through the windows or enter and have a drink.

By six o'clock, as Carter expected, they got bored with the game and just waited in the sedan.

It was then Carter decided to school them a little.

"Another bar, senhor?" the driver asked wearily.

"Yes," Carter said, "let's go back to that first one."

The bar was about eight blocks from the hotel. When the driver stopped, Carter pressed a fat wad of bills into his hand.

"You've been a very understanding man. That's it for today, but I do need one more thing."

"Sim?"

"I won't be coming out of this one. But I want you to sit out here for about a half hour before you leave. Got that?"

"Sim," the driver said with a shrug, and picked up his magazine.

Very little had changed inside in the past two hours. The customers were the same, just a little drunker. The bartender polished the same glasses, and the same two girls were on duty, a redhead in a red dress peeling, the blonde watching her at the bar.

Carter slid onto a stool three down from the blonde. The redhead spotted him and moved down the runway.

Her red dress was resting on a chair at the end of the runway and she was now down to panties and a halter. She had a full-blown figure and she danced and strutted with a certain grace as she whipped aside the panties to expose a spangled G-string.

Carter glanced up and the halter came off to reveal what seemed like naked breasts, the net bra being almost invisible. There was a long moment when she faced him at the bar with wide-flung arms and a big smile. Then the spot went off and she relaxed in darkness. An instant later she had picked up the red dress and, holding it in front of her, hurried down the steps toward some black curtains.

The blonde had moved down to the stool beside Carter's. She pressed her thigh against him and smiled.

"Change your mind?"

"Maybe," Carter said, returning the smile.

The bartender remembered him as well, and brought him a light scotch. Carter took a sip, not really wanting it.

"Buy me a drink?" the blonde purred.

"How much do you make off drinks?"

"Half," she said.

Carter slid a twenty under her arm. She looked at it, then him.

"Not here," she said. "My room, across the street."

Carter shook his head. "Is there a back way out of here?"

"You in trouble?" she whispered, her eyes wide.

"Nothing bad. I just need to shake a couple of bad boys out front."

She slipped the twenty into her cleavage. "See those curtains back there?"

"Yeah."

"Wait a couple of minutes and then follow me." She slipped off the stool and sauntered away.

Carter waited, sipping the weak drink, then dropped a bill on the bar and followed. The blonde was waiting just inside the curtains.

"This way, through our dressing room."

Carter moved in behind her down the dark hall and through another set of curtains. The redhead, still more or less naked, sat with her feet up on her makeup table, reading a magazine and drinking a Coke. She never looked up as Carter came through.

"This door leads to the alley behind the club." She opened it and pressed a piece of paper into his hand. "You ever need anything else, the name is Gila."

"Thanks."

Carter stepped into the alley and the door closed behind him. He started to throw the slip of paper away, then thought, *You never know,* and pocketed it.

He walked in a wide circle to the rear of the hotel. Just in case they had another watcher in the lobby, he might as well confuse them all the way.

The freight elevator operator took him up to his floor, after Carter explained that he was in a hurry and didn't want to go around to the front entrance. The operator accepted the excuse and a tip with a good-humored smile.

His key was at the desk, so he prowled up and down the corridor, calling softly for the maid. Finally she popped out of a tiny closetlike room, blushing and rubbing her eyes sleepily. She unlocked his door, smiling oddly now, and when she strolled away the grin lingered on her full, handsome face.

Carter shrugged, pushing open the door, and then he realized that the lights were on and smelled the tang of fresh cigarette smoke.

She was sitting in a low armchair, her slender legs resting on an ottoman. She uncoiled and moved toward him, her hand held out.

From her neck to the soles of her feet, she was covered in smoky black chiffon, so thin it was almost as if the pigmentation of her skin had darkened and she was nude. Her long golden hair was done up in two thick braids and wound around her head like a *moujik* on market day. A gold chain was slung low around her hips, and dangling from it was a large gold medallion encrusted with semiprecious stones which, when it wasn't swinging, served as an impromptu fig leaf.

"You never called me." Her voice was husky, low, the accent Slavic.

"I've been busy," Carter said in Huzel's thick accent, his body tense as he took her hand.

"I am Verna Rashkin."

Carter relaxed, dropped her hand, and stripped off his jacket. "How the hell did you get in?"

"I told the maid I was your friend."

That explained the grin, Carter thought. "What can I do for you?"

She took a cigarette from her bag and fitted it into a holder. "I would like to propose a merger."

"What kind of a merger?" Carter asked. She waved the holder around a bit, and when Carter didn't produce his lighter she lit the cigarette herself, making a production out of it.

"It is stupid for the three of us to bid wildly against each other for Bolivar's gems."

"Three of us?"

"Don't tell me you don't know Bourlein is here."

"I didn't," Carter lied.

"Who else but the three of us could handle a buy like this?"

"True," Carter said.

She moved forward until the tips of her breasts almost touched his shirt. "As long as the two of us are bidding together, we can outflank Bourlein."

"What if it's a closed bid, one time only?"

"Then we find out what Bourlein's bid is."

"How do we do that?" Carter asked.

"There are ways," she answered languidly. "The important thing is that we don't run the bid up on each other. Once the gems go to one of us, we split with each other."

"I don't like partners."

Her arms came around his neck and the hard points of her breasts pressed his chest. "Don't be a fool," she whispered. "We can be more than partners."

The kiss started off slowly enough, but it soon became feverish. Her lips were soft, knowing, insistent, drawing his tongue to meet hers in a flame-flicking duel. Her small teeth were sharp, playful; they caught his lip for an instant and he tasted blood. He bit back and she broke the kiss.

"You play rough," she whispered. She leaned back and looked at him from eyes that were eager. Her tongue darted out to lick a drop of bright scarlet from her lip.

"I'll play any way you want. Just lay down the rules and fill me in on them."

"I like it rough." She nipped at his earlobe and laughed when he pulled away. "Is that too rough for you?"

"Not at all." Carter looked straight into her eyes and closed one hand over her breast. He purposely squeezed it harder than was necessary. "How about you?"

"The rougher the better." She closed her hand over his so that the pressure increased. Then her nails raked the back of his hand and came away tipped with his blood.

With casual cruelty, Carter slapped her open-handed across the face. It left a red mark on her cheek. Her eyes glowed briefly and then closed. "Again!" she sighed. "Do it again!"

"No," Carter growled. "You like it too much."

"Bastard!"

She swung, but Carter caught her wrist. With his other hand he picked up her purse and guided her to the door.

"What are you doing?" she cried.

"Showing you the door, lady. Bolivar's no idiot. He sniffs collusion between us, we'd never see home again."

He opened the door and showed her into the hallway.

"You're a fool," she fumed.

Carter slammed the door and checked his shirt. A few drops of blood—hers or his, or both—had stained the front of it.

"Bitch," he hissed, and peeled out of it. In the bath

he got his bleeding lip to clot and then pulled on a fresh shirt. He was retying his tie when the phone rang. "Yes?"

"Herr Huzel?" The voice spoke German with a heavy French accent. Carter could hear a peculiar background noise, a whirring, mechanical sound.

"Yes."

"I would like to meet with you."

"Oh?" Carter's voice was tentative.

"I believe I can be of great use to you."

"In what way?"

"I can help you. In your business."

Carter frowned. "What do you know about my business?"

There was a tense laugh from the voice at the other end. "I know all about your business, I'm afraid."

"I see. You have a villa to sell?"

There was a roaring laugh from the other end of the line. "A villa? Dear me, you are an amusing man. Shall we say, Hernando's at eight?"

The line went dead. Carter hung up, shaking his head.

It didn't take a genius to guess that the man on the phone had been Ravel Bourlein. Another good guess was that Bourlein, like Verna Rashkin, wanted to make a deal.

Nice little group of people, he thought. Then thought again. *Or a nest of vipers*.

TEN

Hernando's occupied the basement of a condo high-rise overlooking the ocean. It came with a canopy over the sidewalk and a doorman who resembled a solemn bear in a heavy coat with brass buttons.

He bowed Carter into a small gilt-and-red-velvet lobby. There was a leather-padded door leading to the inside of the restaurant.

Carter was surprised to find the place was large and comfortably appointed. There were round white tables scattered around the room, and the chairs were upholstered in the same red velvet as the lobby. The subdued lighting came from recessed ceiling fixtures. Taken as a whole, the room seemed rather French and was somehow soothing.

The maître d' was instantly at Carter's side. "Table for one?"

"I'm with a party. My name is Huzel."

112

"Of course, this way."

Carter followed him toward a rear booth. It was occupied by an enormous man in a white suit and a voluptuous brunette with a pouty mouth in a bland face.

"Ah, Huzel, welcome!" For his size the man was quick on his feet. His handshake was limp with a sweaty palm.

Again Carter relaxed. Obviously the man had never met Fabian Huzel face to face. "Bourlein."

The same guttural laugh Carter had heard on the phone. "I thought you would know it was me. Allow me to introduce my secretary, Nanette."

The woman rolled her eyes up and cased Carter. She seemed to like what she saw. A little life came into her face.

"Bonjour."

"Mademoiselle," Carter said with a slight bow, and the two men took their seats.

"A drink, senhor?"

"A double scotch, neat," Carter said, and the maître d' glided away.

"It is good to meet you at last," Bourlein said, spreading pâté thickly on a chunk of bread.

Carter's drink came and he sipped it, watching the jowly man over the rim of the glass. "Is it?"

"Of course. I admire good competition, and you and I are the best."

"What about Verna Rashkin?"

Bourlein dismissed the name with a wave of his hand. "A ruthless amateur. The woman uses her sex instead of finesse and good business practices."

"She paid a visit to my room," Carter said.

"I expected she would," the fat man chuckled. "It is her way. Did she try and seduce you?"

"Yes."

"And?"

"None of your business."

"Then you didn't succumb. Good."

The brunette asked to be excused; her makeup needed tending. Bourlein let her out of the booth and resumed his seat.

"I suppose the bitch wanted to make a deal with you?"

"She did," Carter said, noting out of the corner of his eye that Nanette had made a detour past the powder room to a bank of pay phones. "Probably the same deal you're about to offer me."

"Astute," the big man said, and smiled slyly. "Of course, my deal is much better."

"Oh?" Carter lit a cigarette. The brunette finished her call and disappeared into the ladies' room.

"I calculate the resale on Bolivar's gems at somewhere around sixty million. It will take time, a great deal of time."

"True."

"I propose to give you five million now, this very night. A tidy profit for your trip, and you don't even have to be involved."

Carter seemed to think it over seriously. The brunette returned. Carter tried to read her eyes, but there was nothing there.

"What if you are still outbid by Rashkin?" he said.

The smile was oily and cocksure. "I won't be. I happen to know that the bitch has been able to raise financing for only half the deal."

"So," Carter mused, "that's why she came to me."

"Of course. What do you say?"

"No deal," Carter replied, sliding from the booth. "I already have buyers. No matter what you bid, Bourlein, I can do better."

The jowly jaw set and the dark eyes became stones. "I don't like to lose, Huzel."

"Tough shit," Carter growled. "Thanks for the drink. I think I'll have dinner at my hotel. I'd rather eat alone."

Carter turned and left the restaurant. There were no cabs on the street. A block to his left, he saw the black sedan. His two watchdogs had picked him up again when he left the hotel.

Then he spotted the second sedan, just like the first, with two men slouching in the front seat.

He chuckled to himself.

Bolivar was watching them all.

There was a larger, more heavily traveled avenue below, nearer the beach. Carter crossed the street and walked down two flights of narrow stone steps.

He was almost to the bottom when he heard footsteps, one man, behind him. He quickened his descent. Two more were waiting, both breathing heavily. They must have run down from the street above to intercept him.

The two figures moved closer, became faces, bodies, young faces that were hard, young bodies that moved with easy litheness.

"We want your money, senhor," one of them hissed.

"Give us trouble and it will be rougher," said the other.

Carter backed against the pipe railing, curling his

fingers around it. Behind him, the footsteps stopped.

Carter took a roll of bills from his pocket and tossed it onto the concrete walk. "That's all I have."

That stopped them for an instant. The two in front of him looked at each other in a quizzical way, then the leader bent down. He put the bills in his pocket and moved forward again.

"I think maybe you got more," he snarled.

There was a small parking area for the beach. Carter left the rail and moved to one of the cars. The one on the steps came all the way down, and all three of them advanced.

Carter was against the car now, his back to the fender. He heard the flat slap of a sap being hit against the palm of a hand, and his eyes found the weapon in the hand of the third one of the trio. The other two wore gloves on their right hands. The lead one grinned with obscene anticipation and moved forward, the other two following.

Carter waited, gauging, measuring, letting split seconds tick off, and then he exploded into action.

Using the fender of the car as a lever, he kicked out with both feet, twisting his body at the same time. The blow caught the first one full in the abdomen, and Carter heard his gasp of pain as he doubled over, went down on one knee. The other two rushed forward, expecting him to stand and swing back. Instead, he lifted himself against the fender and flung himself backward across the hood of the car. He heard the two crash against the fender as he reached the opposite side of the hood.

"Get him, dammit!" one snarled viciously. "Kill the bastard!"

Carter slipped from the hood to the ground, landing on his feet as the pair came around the front. Out of the corner of his eye he saw the third one starting to pull himself to his feet on the other side. The two others slowed, then started toward him again, and he caught the dull glint of metal in the first one's hand. He backed, and they continued forward.

He had toyed with the idea of carrying the Beretta, and then at the last minute had left it hidden in his room.

He regretted it now.

One of them had a short length of pipe. The leader had his sap. To Carter's surprise, it was the third one who came at him with his bare hands.

Carter didn't wait for him to swing. He stepped forward and hit him just below the ribs. It was like shoving his fist into a concrete wall. Then it was his turn. Before Carter could get out of the way, he caught one high on the cheek. It felt as if he'd been hit by a two-by-four. Part of his face went numb, and there was a warm trickle down his cheek as he fell backward to the ground.

He looked up and saw a foot swinging at him. He rolled to one side, grabbed the foot, and heaved as hard as he could. For a brief moment he towered above Carter, tottering on his feet. Then he went down like an axed tree. His breath whistled as it was forced from his lungs.

But then the other two came on like a pair of trucks. The sap caught Carter high on the shoulder. The end of the pipe went into his gut. He rolled and came up swinging. He dropped one with a kick to the groin, but the other two were in close and working him over.

It was then he knew that they weren't trying to kill him. They were too precise. Their intent was to cripple him, and they were doing a good job of it.

He was sinking to his knees, when the blows suddenly stopped. He got one eye open and saw the reason.

Chunky and the young one, Carter's watchers, were methodically pistol-whipping all three of his assailants. It was over in seconds and the young one came over and helped Carter to his feet.

"Are you all right, Senhor Huzel?"

"Sore, a little bloody, but I'll live."

"The beach is very dangerous at night," he replied. "Many muggers."

"I don't think so," Carter grunted. "You work for Bolivar?"

"*Sim*," the man said. "We are told to watch over you."

"So watch me," Carter hissed, and staggered forward to where the leader lay prone in front of a car. He rolled the youth over and went through his pockets.

He located the wad of bills he had tossed on the ground, and a second wad, even thicker. He shoved all the bills into his own pocket and stood.

"Bourlein still in the restaurant?"

The young man shook his head. "He and his woman left just after you."

"Is he at the Leme?"

"*Sim.*"

"Give me a ride back to the hotel," Carter said, already heading for the stairs.

Carter skirted the lobby and signaled the bell captain to follow him toward the elevators.

"You need a doctor, senhor?"

"No. I need a bucket of ice and Senhor Ravel Bourlein's room number, pronto." He gave the man a bill and pushed the button for his floor.

In his room he repaired his face and examined the body bruises. The skin was already turning purple, but nothing was broken.

There was a rap on the door and he let the bellman in. "Bourlein?"

"He is in a suite, Twelve-twelve."

Carter gave him another hefty tip and shoved him out the door. He built a scotch and drank it while he changed clothes. Then he slipped the Beretta into his belt and took the elevator to the twelfth floor.

"Who is it?"

"Bell captain, senhor," Carter said, in a high voice. "You have a cable."

The door opened a crack and Carter shouldered it wide. He gave Bourlein two good shots in the middle of his flab and then a hard one behind the ear on his way down.

He kicked the door shut, locked it, and dragged the fat man by his ankles into the suite.

The woman, Nanette, stood naked except for a pair of bikini panties, her mouth round in a silent scream.

"Not a sound," Carter growled. "Get some ice and a wet towel."

She nodded dumbly, eyes bulging, and moved into the small kitchen area.

"Move it!" Carter barked. "I'm in a hurry."

The woman had gotten her breath and a little nerve back. "What the hell do you want?"

"A little talk with him . . . bring the stuff."

returned, her vast bosoms jiggling and swaying. She tried a hesitant smile, but one look at Carter's face and she cut the act and thrust the ice and the wet towel at him.

"Over here," Carter said.

To her astonishment, Carter gathered a fistful of Bourlein's shirtfront and jerked him to a sitting position, then lifted him into a chair. He motioned her around the chair.

"Rub the back of his neck with the ice."

"Let me get some clothes on," she whimpered.

Carter looked at her, stepped forward, and slapped her. She went sideways, airborne. Her vision dimmed with stars behind her eyes. She felt herself jerked upright by her hair, held there by the aching, stinging strain on her scalp until her wobbly knees found strength and she stood. Just as she got her wind, the throbbing pain along the left side of her face began occupying her mind. She tried twisting away and the grip in her hair tightened. Carter slapped her again, and she shrieked.

"No, no!" she cried.

"Good," Carter said. "I don't like it either." He turned loose his grip wound in her long dark hair and shoved. She stumbled across the room and fell in Bourlein's lap.

"Up!" he hissed, and she shot to her feet. "Use that ice on the back of his neck."

She squealed and sprawled as she reached for the ice, got it, and scrambled to her feet. She tilted Bourlein's head forward and began rubbing his neck with the ice.

Carter went to work on his face with the towel, back and forth, one side, then the other. Bourlein began moving, then moaning. Finally he cried out and jerked upright.

"What the—" he gasped.

Carter's face was inches from his. "Three bad local lads tried to bust my head tonight," he hissed.

"I don't know anything about it . . ."

"You ass. You tried to make a deal. I didn't dance. So you tried to put me in a hospital so I couldn't be there to make a bid."

"You're crazy."

"I don't think so," Carter said. "You had big boobs here call the lads from the restaurant and give them my description. There was no deal. You just wanted to get me out of the way."

"No, I swear . . ."

"Bullshit." Carter looked up at the trembling woman. "Right?"

She gulped and then nodded, once.

Carter dropped the towel, drew the Beretta, and crammed the barrel between Bourlein's fat lips, shattering teeth. The man reared back and the woman squealed. Carter shot her a look, and she quieted instantly.

"You hear me, Bourlein? Blink your eyes if you do," he growled.

Bourlein blinked. He tried leaning forward, making gagging sounds.

"Swallow it," Carter commanded. "Swallow it all, you bastard." He rammed the gun barrel hard, feeling the high, ribbed front sight rip the roof of Bourlein's mouth, rammed until the trigger guard rested against his fat lips, inches of cold steel gun barrel gagging him, choking him, his eyes bulging.

The woman kept making tiny mewling sounds, like those of a kitten in pain.

"Let me give you your itinerary for the next few hours, fat man. You're going to call the desk and have them get you a car. Then you're going to check out and you're going to drive to São Paolo. Bolivar's watchdogs will follow you. They won't know what's going on, and by the time they figure it out you and Nanny here will be on the first flight. You got that? I don't give a shit where the flight goes, just so it's out of the country and you're on it. Nod if you understand."

Bourlein didn't move. He just stared pure hate at Carter from his beady eyes.

The Killmaster cocked the Beretta. "So long, fat man."

The head started nodding.

Carter wiped the barrel on Bourlein's shirt, stuck the gun back in his belt, and headed for the door, where he paused.

"If I see you at Rancho Corinto, Bourlein, I'll kill you."

He took the elevator to the fourth floor and knocked on 417. He heard the padding of bare feet and then Verna Rashkin's sleepy voice.

"Who is it?"

"Fabian Huzel. Open up."

The door opened and Carter slid inside. She backed away and he kicked it closed. Her hair was tousled and she wore only a sheer black nightgown, low in front, that stopped at midthigh. Under the black garment's gauzy transparency, her smooth pink-and-whiteness gleamed and shimmered as she moved. The black material rustled around her, more like a dark mist than a cover, heightening her nakedness rather than concealing it. But in the end her flesh glowed with blinding incandescence.

"What do you want?" she whispered.

"You made a proposition a little while ago. Is it still on?"

Suddenly she was bright-eyed and alert. "It is."

"Then you've got a deal," Carter said.

"You won't regret it. I'll bet Bourlein's bid as soon as we get to Rancho Corinto."

"From Nanette?"

Her eyes narrowed. "How did you know?"

"I didn't," Carter said. "I guessed. You'd never get to Bourlein. It had to be his whore."

She shrugged. "Nanette's tired of him, and I offered her a good retirement plan."

"I upped your offer," Carter said. "Bourlein won't be bidding. It's all ours."

She couldn't conceal her surprise. "How did you do that?"

"Proper conversation," Carter said. "Aren't you forgetting something?"

"What?"

"The rest of your offer."

Her lips parted showing sharp, white teeth. "All night," she whispered. "I'm going to make love to you all night."

Her hands slid down her thighs, to the hem of the nightie just above her knees. Still moving slowly, she raised it, revealing her long, slender legs inch by quivering inch. When it was at a point just below the juncture of her legs, she swayed her body around so that her back was to him. The nightie inched up higher and now he could see the firm, high globes of her buttocks. Her rhythmical movement quickened. The muscles of her derrière rippled and the flesh began to jump with a sort of erotic frenzy.

Then she quickly pulled the garment over her head, flipped it away, and turned to face him.

He let his eyes roam over her body, at the firmness and the maturity of her breasts, the sweeping curve of her hips. She seemed to delight in feeling his eyes on her, for she lifted her long hair with the tips of her fingers and turned around slowly, displaying herself.

"Well?" she murmured.

"Nice," Carter said, "damn nice. See you in the morning."

"What?" she cried.

"Just wanted to see if your word was good," he said over his shoulder as he let himself out. "'Night."

ELEVEN

Carter was the first one down the next morning. Young-and-lean and short-and-chunky were waiting for him in the lobby. They looked tense, so Carter was sure they had gotten the word on Bourlein and his busty brunette friend.

The young one grabbed Carter's bag. "The car is in front, Senhor Huzel. The hotel bill has been taken care of by Senhor Bolivar."

"Nice of him."

Carter followed him out the door. The little sedan had been replaced by a Mercedes limo. Carter crawled in the back. Seconds later, short-and-chunky emerged with Verna Rashkin. She joined Carter in the rear with a smirk on her face.

"I didn't notice your face last night. You look like hell."

Carter smiled. "I feel fine."

Actually, he was sore as hell. The crack across the bridge of his nose had blackened both his eyes, which were a puffy lavender-brown. His lips had swollen, giving his face an even more prognathous look than normal. The tape above his cheekbones, over his eye, and at his ear made him look like the comic-strip caricature of a man lately thrown out of a beer hall.

The limo pulled into traffic and they were silent all the way to the airport.

The plane was a twin-engine Bonanza, not new but in excellent shape. The bags were loaded and Carter buckled himself in. He was surprised when the woman seated herself as far from him as possible. He wasn't surprised when the two watchers crawled in and took seats in the rear.

The pilot didn't even turn around. He already had the off-side engine humming. The hatch was barely secure when the second engine burped to life and the tail swung around.

In no time they were in the takeoff area and turned into the wind. He spoke into his headpiece and advanced the throttles.

The takeoff was smooth and they climbed about five hundred feet per minute. The pilot began a 90-degree left turn, followed by a 45-degree right turn, in order to leave the traffic pattern. He leveled off at three thousand feet. The green and brown earth dropped away below, and they headed toward the never-ending blue sky.

The Bonanza followed the ribbon of coastline below. From this altitude it looked like a chemist's bizarre experiment—browns, greens, blues, and grays moving between sunlight and shadow. The shoreline itself often became obscured by mountains dropping into the water.

About twenty minutes after takeoff there was another bank to the right and they headed inland. Carter looked down at the dense jungle and shuddered slightly. He hoped he wouldn't have to come back out on foot.

Short-and-chunky played steward. Verna Rashkin wanted a Bloody Mary. Carter declined anything and leaned back on the headrest. He forced himself to half-doze for the next hour, until he felt the plane start its descent.

The flaps came down. They banked 45 degrees into the wind and swooped over the shimmering asphalt runway. Mountains and water diminished as the plane descended. The landing gear dropped the wheels down, and then the plane was bumping and squeaking along sun-softened pitch seams. The pilot taxied right down the runway to the first Quonset-style hangar. The crackling, robotlike voice from the control tower ceased.

The pilot turned in his seat. "This is Paranavi. The helicopter will take you the rest of the way."

They scrambled down the steps and under the wing of the Bonanza toward a blue-and-red helicopter whose rotor was already beginning to turn.

Once inside, Carter removed a pair of dark glasses from the pocket of his jacket and put them on against the glare in the helicopter's bubble.

"Is it far?" he asked the pilot.

"Not far," the man replied, pointing toward the mountains. "Up there, maybe twenty minutes."

It was nineteen. The chopper swooped low, flying over a large estate surrounded by mountains. There were several barns, fields of grazing horses and cattle, small barracklike houses, and a lake.

The chopper roared over the outbuildings and Carter

heard a gasp from across the aisle. He looked, and saw why Verna had gasped.

The house was awesome, a huge, rambling affair built of stone and glass. It was set directly against a jut of mountain rock that provided perfect protection from the rear. To the right were the garages, servants' quarters, and accommodation for guards, ten of whom Bolivar kept in permanent residence, on a rotating basis. The stables for the horses were to the left, where there was more land available. The center of the huge winding drive was permanently watered, and therefore green, garden area, with a playing fountain and a blaze of flowers.

"He must own the whole valley!" Verna exclaimed.

"Probably," Carter replied dryly, "and most of the mountains as well."

The helicopter landed on the lawn and the engine was killed at once. They stepped to the ground to be met by a striking blond woman, so tall that her eyes were level with Carter's. She sported a voluptuous, hourglass figure in a white crocheted sweater of an open-weave stitch, and jade green, silk slacks. A matching green cardigan draped over her shoulders obstructed most of the view. The only jewelry she had on was a large square-cut emerald on the third finger of her left hand. Its color matched almost exactly the color of her eyes. She was beautiful—ten years and twenty pounds less and she must have been spectacular.

"I am Eva, Senhor Bolivar's housekeeper. Anything you need while you are here, do not hesitate to ask me. Senhor Bolivar is hunting at the moment. He will join us for dinner. This way, please. I will show you to your rooms." Her accent was Bavarian and it was heavy.

They moved obediently behind her, Carter expecting at any time to hear The *Ride of the Valkyries*.

Up close, inside the house was even more immense and awe-inspiring. It was two stories high and shaped like an L, with the short arm cantilevered out over a sloping landscaped hill. The short arm was only a single story, and comprised the living room, with the terrace right alongside; at right angles was the long arm, two floors of bedrooms, a dining room, and probably a study as well. Carter's room was on the second floor, near the bend in the L.

The entire building was constructed from glass and stone, and inside and out, it was sharp, clean, bare, and smooth. The unsparing, almost harsh quality of the lines was broken by the occasional use of bricks to add texture, and the low stone walls that ran around the house, screening it from the view of anyone for miles.

"This is your room, Herr Huzel. You, Fräulein, are across the hall. Your bags will be up shortly. The pool is in the center courtyard, if you care to swim."

She clomped back down the hall and disappeared.

Carter looked at Verna. Her mouth was open. "Awesome, isn't it, in the middle of nowhere?"

"It is that."

"Care to pool it?" Carter asked.

"I think I'll sit in a tub."

"Suit yourself."

Inside the room, Carter went over it. In ten minutes he found three bugs. From his window he could see a brace of four armed guards patrolling beyond the walls around the house.

Short-and-chunky entered the room without knocking and dropped Carter's bag on the bed.

"I searched your luggage," he grunted.

"My God, it talks," Carter exclaimed.

"And took your gun."

"I figured you would," the Killmaster said with a smile.

Much to Carter's surprise, the swimming pool was highly populated, all women. They were predominantly blond, and German was the common language. Only the bottoms of bikinis were worn.

He dived into the pool and after five fast lengths got rid of the kinks from the previous night's fight. Feeling better, he climbed out and sat on a stool at the outdoor bar.

"A drink, mein Herr?" Carter turned. He was tall, built like a tank, and very Aryan. "My name is Bernard."

"Yeah," Carter replied. *"Ein Bier.* All these lovelies Bolivar's guests?"

Bernard shrugged. "In a way. They are flown in for a month at a time, two or three times a year. They liven up the parties and keep the guards happy."

Carter sipped his beer. Bolivar, he thought, probably got a lot of loyalty out of his troops.

A well-built girl parked a well-built thigh on a stool two along. She ordered an orange juice and smiled at Carter.

"You should try it with vodka. It brightens the day," he suggested.

"I don't drink. You're German?"

He nodded. "But I live in Amsterdam."

"I live in Bremerhaven. I went to the university."

"Went . . . ?"

"I ran out of money."

"Oh," Carter said. "And that's why you're here?"

"That's why I'm here. See you."

She walked around the pool and Carter watched her until she entered the house. He turned back to Bernard.

"I understand Senhor Bolivar is hunting. What's good up in the mountains?"

"Men," Bernard replied calmly. "Rebels. It's been a good week. He has bagged five."

"Good sport," Carter said, managing a smile.

He watched the bevy of beauties a while longer, and then wandered into the house. There was a maid here and a maid there, but no one seemed inclined to stop him so he kept wandering.

At the far end of the first floor, he heard radio chatter and a teletype. That would figure. If Bolivar never left the place, he would need some kind of constant communication with the outside world.

He climbed to the second floor and continued to move around until he found a trapdoor that went up to the roof. He had already guessed that there would be access to the roof from the inside, and was elated he had found it so soon.

He moved on through the rest of the rooms until he entered what he assumed was Bolivar's office. It was book-lined, the desk a fine piece of English walnut, a fireplace mantel adorned with carvings of horses. The top of the desk was clean save for the usual ashtrays and pens. The top drawer was locked. He found a letter opener and, working crudely, snapped the lock open and yanked the drawer out. He sat down in the chair and began to rifle through the papers and file folders, moving from the top drawer to those at the side.

What he found was enlightening. Bolivar was rich, but he was also very overextended. Vinnick had been wrong about the man's reason for wanting to liquidate the jewels.

Bolivar needed the cash.

Carter replaced the desk as he had found it and turned to the wall. A large print of a steeplechase hung on the wood-paneled wall. He lifted up one corner, his eyes narrowing, lifted again, and removed the entire print.

The wall safe, neat and flush to the wall, stared back at him. It was an old one, he saw, a combination lock. It would take time and patience to open, he thought ruefully, more than he had now. He put an ear to the dial, turned it carefully, played with its clicks, counting, making mental calculations.

After another minute he knew that, given time, he could crack it.

Just as he replaced the print, he heard footsteps in the hall. He tugged a book from the wall and opened it.

Big Eva came through the door, saw him, and came up short. "You are looking for something, Herr Huzel?"

"*Ja*, a good book to read," he replied, glancing down at the book and then back up to her with a smile. "But everything in here seems to be in Russian."

Eva-the-Amazon had informed them that drinks were at eight, dinner at nine. At eight sharp, Carter descended the stairs. From the great room he heard the sound of music, guitars, drums and marimbas.

He entered the great room to see a three-piece band in a far alcove, and preparations for a huge buffet being made along the opposite wall. There were about twenty people, mostly the young women he had seen by the pool that afternoon. Interspersed among them were a few young, unsmiling men in gray trousers and dark blue blazers. Besides the clothes, each of them had a hard, alert quality to his darting eyes.

Then Carter realized. This was part of the security force, the new stormtroopers. They had no brown shirts or Sam Browne belts, no jackboots, but stormtroopers they were.

He was working his way toward the bar when he saw Sergeant Boris Glaskov alias Enrique Bolivar. He was a bull of a man, with shoulders and arms that stretched his dinner jacket. Despite his relatively short stature, he was a commanding presence, with cropped white hair, the sharp eyes of a condor, and thick, cruel lips.

He was deep in smiling conversation with a woman whose back was partly to Carter. She had a long, lithe figure in a sleeveless, backless, almost frontless white gown, eyes that were black-olive moist and deep. He saw skin, browned and burnished as if dusted by gold, long black hair and a straight nose, full, sensuous lips. He saw a woman who glowed outside and inside, smoldered with a throbbing, pulsating earthiness.

Then he recognized her as the girl from Bremerhaven he had met by the pool that afternoon.

A little makeup, a change of hairstyle, and clothes, he thought, can make a hell of a difference.

He had just reached the bar when Bolivar spotted him and started over.

"What would you care to drink, Herr Huzel?" It was big blond Bernard.

"You have long hours, Bernard."

A shrug. "The compensation is good. Scotch?"

"A double, one cube."

"Herr Huzel, we meet at last." Bolivar didn't offer his hand. He bowed sharply from the waist.

"Senhor Bolivar," Carter said, executing the same bow, "a pleasure."

"We must talk, privately."

"Of course."

"There is a sitting room, this way. Bring your drink."

Carter followed him from the room. Just outside the door they were joined by another man.

"Umberto Grossman," Bolivar explained, "my head of security."

Grossman was tall and athletic, handsome in a heavy way, with slick black hair and an arrogant mouth. He took Carter's measure and then seemed to dismiss him with a nod.

They entered a small sitting room with chairs around a fireplace and not much else. Bolivar waved Carter to one of the chairs, and took the other. Grossman became a statue by the door with his hands in an at-ease position over his crotch.

"I am disappointed, Huzel. I asked you here to negotiate a fortune, and you attempt to do business with two petty thieves." The way he sat in the chair, slightly forward, his hands on the armrests, made him look like a predator.

"You mean Perrez and Raffini, of course."

"Yes."

"I do business wherever there is business. There is always the chance I would lose the bid here, so I thought I might pick up a few baubles from those two for my trouble."

Bolivar accepted this with a scowl. "That brings us

to something else. What happened to Bourlein? I know you had something to do with it."

Carter lit a cigarette and let the smoke slide slowly from each nostril. "I had everything to do with it. He offered me a deal. I turned it down."

"What kind of a deal?"

"A five-million buyout, and I go away. When I refused the deal, he paid to have me hospitalized so I couldn't be here to bid. Really, I think his three hired thugs would have tried to break me up even if I had agreed to the deal. As it turned out, I told him to go away."

"That, too, is interesting," Bolivar said. "Ravel Bourlein is a hard man, ruthless. He doesn't give up easily. How did you convince him?"

Carter glanced at Grossman to make sure he was listening. "I stuck a Beretta down his throat and told him if he showed up here, I would kill him."

"Just a threat like that, and he went away?" Bolivar scoffed.

Carter leaned forward, set his jaw, and lowered his voice. "He knew I meant it. Now, since I am the only bidder, suppose we get on with it. I have to get back to Amsterdam."

Bolivar's eyebrows shot up. "The only bidder . . . ?"

"The Rashkin bitch doesn't have the financing for the entire collection. She wants to rig the bid with me and take half."

From the look on the old man's face, Carter knew Bolivar had not done his homework. It was also a pretty good bet that Bourlein had. Bolivar tried to bluff it through.

"There are other brokers," he said, and shrugged.

"Bullshit," Carter growled, "not for the kind of merchandise you have." From the corner of his eye he saw Grossman take a step forward. He whirled on Bolivar. "Tell your personal goon that if he takes another step I'll rip off his arm and shove it up his ass."

Grossman puffed up like an adder. Bolivar held up a hand to calm him, and then leaned back in his chair, suddenly relaxed. He even smiled, something Carter was sure he did rarely.

"You live up to your reputation, Herr Huzel. I admire a man who has no qualms about achieving his ends. Tell me, would you have actually killed Bourlein?"

"Without a thought."

The black eyes narrowed. "Yes, I believe you would. How much are you prepared to pay?"

"I'll make an offer when I see the collection."

"Fair enough." Bolivar struggled to his feet, using the stick. He commented on it. "Would you believe? Arthritis. I never thought I would grow old."

"Is that why you surround yourself with youth?"

Bolivar's hard eyes bored into Carter's. "Yes, that is part of it. I am a very rich man. But like so many Europeans in South America, I cannot venture too far from this fortress I've built."

"You mean, prison?"

Again Bolivar smiled, but, like the clown, the corners of his mouth turned down. "A way of putting it. So I bring the world to me. The buffet should be served by now. Shall we?"

"Fine," Carter said. "Will I be able to see the collection tomorrow?"

"Perhaps."

They moved into the hall. Just before they entered the room, Bolivar paused.

"By the way, in your travels, have you come across a man named Goldolph . . . Otto Goldolph? He has a daughter named Magda. She is an older woman, I'm told quite beautiful still."

"No, I've never heard the name."

"What about Bittrich . . . Erwin Bittrich?"

Carter stopped, forcing his face into a mask of stone. "I would think that you, of all people, would know that name."

Bolivar matched Carter's look. His hand came up like a claw and grasped the Killmaster's lapel with surprising strength. "Why, Huzel? Why should I know that name?"

Carter became flustered. "Why, because . . ."

"Why?"

"I assume, mein Herr," Carter said, "because of the old days, the glory days."

Bolivar got hold of himself. Vinnick had been right. The man, without stating anything specific, had passed himself off in the South American German community as one of them.

"Yes, the old days, of course. But what of Bittrich?"

"I deal with a great many people," Carter replied. "As you know, discretion is imperative."

"But you know who is who?"

"Yes."

"About Bittrich. Tell me about him. I would consider it a great favor."

Carter gave him a quick rundown of Erwin Bittrich's Nazi career, and ended with, ". . . his last command was the Twenty-first Panzers, stationed in Romania."

If it was possible with his sun-burnished skin, Bolivar's face became flushed and then seemed to lose all color. He swayed slightly on his stick until Grossman grabbed his elbow.

Carter knew why.

Graf von Wassner was intelligence security for the Twenty-first Panzers. As such, he would have reported directly to General Erwin Bittrich.

The ball was rolling, and soon it would gather speed.

TWELVE

The sound of the helicopter warming up awakened Carter. Early-morning sun slanted through the windows, already preparing the room for the day's heat.

He moved off the bed, a bit creakily. Unidentifiable muscles and joints creaked and cracked. His feet hit the floor, and cursing Ravel Bourlein, he shot himself into an upright position and moved across to the windows.

He was just in time to see Bolivar hurry across the grass. Grossman awaited him and gave him a hand into the chopper. The moment the hatch was closed behind the security chief, the machine rose into the air. The tail twisted around and the helicopter headed southwest as it gained altitude.

Not in the direction of Rio or São Paolo, Carter observed, but toward Uruguay, or Argentina.

Bolivar had probably been on the horn all night trying to contact all the old Nazis he had attempted to be-friend through the years.

Would they have the word yet that Otto was looking for von Wassner?

What would Bolivar tell them? He couldn't tell them the truth. He certainly couldn't tell them that he wasn't the real SS Gruppenführer Graf von Wassner. And if he continued with the lie that he had come to South America because of his Nazi ties, the old guard would start to insist on him telling them just what those ties were.

Carter smiled to himself. Bolivar was going to have a very busy day.

He punched the button on the house intercom and ordered coffee. Then he moved into the bathroom. The shower blasted warm and then cold needles through his body, and he felt alive again when he emerged.

Still wet, he climbed into a pair of swim trunks and a thick pool robe he found behind the door.

He found a tray with coffee and croissants on the balcony table. There was also a note on plain but expensive stationery: *Huzel: I have been called away on an important matter. Please forgive me. We will conclude our business tomorrow.*

Tomorrow, Carter thought. Did that mean Bolivar and his chief of security would be gone overnight? He hoped so.

He was on his second cup of coffee and his first cigarette when his bedroom door was thrown open so hard that the inner knob crashed into the wall.

A very irate Verna Rashkin stormed into the room. She wore the same nightie he had seen the previous night. The difference in appearance between then and now was in the flesh beneath and around the nightie.

There were bruises on her arms and shoulders as well as her hips and thighs.

"You pig . . . you bastard!" She said more, but it was so garbled with anger that Carter could make no sense of it.

"Calm down, Verna. Coffee?"

"You told Bolivar I wanted to make a deal with you!"

"That's right."

"You pig . . ."

"You already said that."

She went straight for Carter's eyes with her talons out. He caught one wrist, then the other, and tossed her on the bed. She still struggled, but she was no match for his body weight.

"Did he tell you about it before he took you to bed . . . or after?" Carter said smoothly.

"He's an animal," she cried. "He abused me half the night, and then this morning told me to get out!"

"So that's where the bruises came from."

She nodded. "I'm to be taken back to Rio sometime today."

Carter chuckled. "I thought he dished out your kind of sex. You probably enjoyed every minute of it."

Verna tried to knee him in the crotch, but he took it on the thigh. "Why did you tell him that I didn't have the backing to make a bid?" she hissed.

"Because you don't."

"But how did you know?" She was practically screaming now.

"Because Bourlein told me." Suddenly she went limp. Carter held on for a few seconds to make sure she stayed that way, then released her and stood. "Want some coffee now?"

She nodded. "And a cigarette."

He gave her both and poured himself a fresh cup. "Tell you what I'll do."

"What?" She was sullen now, defeated, but not liking it.

"I'll make this trip worthwhile if we can work a little trade-off."

Her eyes flashed. "I don't do trade-offs with bastards."

"Yes, you do," Carter said, and smiled. "You traded your body to Bolivar last night to get a leg up on me. He just didn't trade back."

She bristled for an instant longer, then her shoulders sagged. "What do you want?"

"I want you to stick around. I'll clear it with Bolivar, and I'll make it worth your while."

She was intrigued but she didn't jump right in with both feet. "What will you tell him?"

"That I need a second opinion on the jewels... weight, authenticity, the American market."

Carter kept his eyes out the window, staring at the women playing water polo in the pool. He also held his breath until he got an answer. Verna Rashkin didn't know it, but her skill in authenticating the stones would be invaluable. He was fair with a jeweler's glass, but not in her league. If Bolivar tried to toss in some good paste, she could spot it.

She was in front of him then, the anger gone from her large eyes and replaced with dollar signs. She took a deep drag on her cigarette, parted her lips, and let the smoke curl out slowly over her moving tongue like a long kiss.

"How much?" she murmured.

"Enough to make the trip worthwhile."

"That's not enough."

"That's all you're going to get. Let me know, I'm going for a swim."

He left her and headed down to the pool. The helicopter was landing and most of the women were headed for the house. He saw Bremerhaven doing laps, and dived in to join her.

"Good morning," he called.

"Not really," she replied, rolling into an easy backstroke.

"Oh?"

They hit the side of the pool, crawled out, and sat. "Big Eva told us this morning that the chopper would take us in shifts over to Paranavi, then on to Rio."

"Anything odd about that?"

"I suppose not," she said. "It's just that we were supposed to be here for a couple more weeks. Well, I'd better get packed. Nice meeting you."

"*Ja*, the same."

Carter watched her walk around the pool and then into the house.

Bolivar was clearing the decks. It could only mean that he was expecting trouble and he wanted no one on the scene who might carry word of it to the outside world.

Carter smiled to himself.

Otto had done a good job of tapping into Rio's underground information pipeline.

He ordered breakfast and ate it by the pool. When he was finished, he spread out on a chaise in a position to watch the guards move around. They were all armed now, and they seemed more alert than they had been the previous day. Now and then he spotted some of them on horseback riding the outer fringes of the estate.

By noon the helicopter had made three trips and was loading a fourth time.

"Herr Huzel?"

Carter looked up. It was the Amazon, Big Eva, and she had fire in her eyes. *"Ja?"*

"I have been instructed to put Fräulein Rashkin on the helicopter this morning."

"I know. She told me."

"She refuses to go. She tells me to talk to you."

"That's right. I've decided to put her on my personal payroll for a while."

"I cannot do that. I was told—"

"I will explain it to Senhor Bolivar."

"I cannot do that. I was told—"

"What are you, a machine?" Carter barked. "She stays. I'll take care of it."

For a moment he thought she was going to throw him into the pool. They had a staring match, and finally she backed down and stalked off.

Carter took the sun for another hour and then returned to the house. He searched out Eva.

"Fräulein Rashkin and I will go for a ride this afternoon."

"That is impossible. I have been told—"

"Inform the stables that we'll be down there in half an hour."

He left her stuttering, and climbed the stairs to rap on Verna's door. It opened at once.

"Get dressed, we're going riding."

Her mouth twisted into a grimace. "I hate horses."

"You need the air," he growled. "Half an hour."

He entered his own room, took a quick shower, and

dressed. Verna was ready when he knocked on her door again, and they walked down to the stables.

"Why do you want to ride?" she groused, almost running to keep up with his pace.

"To commune with nature."

The stableman was a grisled old Indian who said everything in grunts. They were both barely mounted when he disappeared back into the building.

They had scarcely left the main compound when a mounted guard fell in behind them. Carter could see two more tracking them in a parallel line to their right and left.

"What do you know about Bolivar?" Carter asked.

She shrugged. "What's to know? He's a Nazi who got out when the getting was good."

"How did he first contact you?"

"I do a lot of business in Spain and Portugal. It was through a third party." She glanced at him. "Why the third degree?"

"No particular reason," Carter replied. "Have you sold much of his stuff?"

"A few small pieces. I didn't know until a few weeks ago that he had this big a horde. He sent me a shopping list, invited me to bid."

Carter was silent for a few seconds, and then asked, "Why do you suppose he's bailing out now?"

"You mean you don't know?" she asked, obviously surprised at his question.

"You tell me," he said.

"I only know rumors, but I've heard that he was pretty heavy into oil speculation when the bottom dropped out. Also, the new government in Brasilia isn't as easy on alien residents as the former administration.

He probably wants cash in case he has to run."

Carter nodded. "That's about the way I figure it."

They reached the perimeter of the estate and made a wide swing through the hills. At the lake, a mounted guard would let them go no farther.

It made no difference.

Carter had seen everything he needed to see.

It was one in the morning and the house was quiet as a tomb when Carter slipped from his room. He walked to where he had seen the trapdoor and gently pulled the ladder down. It moved quietly on its oiled springs.

He climbed and pulled the ladder up after him. He lay flat, moving back from the door, a motionless shape under the stars. He crawled across the roof on his belly. At the edge, he rolled over and toe-walked the stones along the wall, grasping the drainpipe with his hands.

At the rim of the L, he dropped from the second-story roof to the first. There was some sound but not enough to raise any alarm.

A huge old tree practically abutted the roof above the kitchen. He got to the ground limb by limb, and melted at once into the shadows.

It took him nearly a half hour to crawl through the compound, get over the wall and around the stables. Twice he had to curl into a ball in the shadows and await passing guards.

At last he reached the edge of the rain forest. He used footpaths for the first two hundred yards, but it was still difficult moving through a dark tunnel with the thick vegetation blocking any hint of the moon and stars.

It was dark now, very dark, not with the blackness of

the night, but with the almost total absence of any infiltrating light. Only the immediate area around him, a few feet, no more, was visible at all. When he stopped to rest he could feel the dampness caress him like a fleshy hand.

Then suddenly the forest was behind him and he was in a clearing with the lake directly in front of him.

He stripped to his shorts and hid his clothes and shoes against a huge tree. Then he got his bearings from the stars and slid into the inky water.

The lake was shaped like a large half-moon. He took to the water close to the center on the concave side. It was about three hundred yards across, and he alternated his strokes to save his strength.

He had scarcely pulled himself out on the other side when Otto, in green fatigues, his Bittrich disguise cast aside, slithered from the trees.

"You're only ten minutes late. Good man. This way."

Wordlessly, Carter followed him into the jungle, where a short, wiry man awaited.

"This is Jorge," Otto said. "Good man. All four of them are."

Carter nodded. Jorge grunted and took the lead.

"How far?" Carter asked.

"About a mile," Otto replied. "Jorge knows this area like the back of his hand. There are ruins of an old mission. We've made camp there."

Somehow, Jorge found paths through the trees and vines. In minutes they were in a little hollow. And then they were in a stone-walled compound. Because of the ever-present forest, constantly growing, Carter hadn't recognized the stones until he was among them.

Likewise, he didn't see the light of the fire until he

was practically on it. Lorena was crouched beside it, the light dancing off the fine bones of her face.

She stood the moment she saw Carter. "Thank God," she whispered. "We were afraid you wouldn't be able to get through."

"It was fairly easy," Carter said, brushing his lips across her cheek. "They're watching from the outside in. Where are the others?"

"Out there, watching, just in case," Otto said, opening a flask and passing it to Carter. "How goes it so far?"

Carter drank, letting the liquor warm his belly, and sat down between them. "The Erwin Bittrich ruse worked. Bolivar is shook up. He flew out this morning. My guess is he'll try to shore up his position."

Otto laughed. "He'll have a bloody hard time of it. The Mossad boys passed me around to several of the contacts they've made. Mostly they were minor people in the government who pass information along to what's left of the old Third Reich."

"And?" Carter said.

"I let it be known that my dear comrade Graf von Wassner was killed by one of his own men."

"Did you name Bolivar?" Carter asked.

"No, but with dates and the Portuguese connection, the right people will put two and two together."

Carter lit a cigarette and stared into the fire. "With any luck, Bolivar will see the handwriting on the wall. Without government sponsorship, he can't stay in Brazil. If the old Nazis won't help him, Argentina and Uruguay will be out."

Lorena hadn't spoken. Now she looked from the fire to Carter. "Which way will he jump?"

"My guess is he'll take what he can salvage and go underground. That could be anywhere."

"Have you seen the jewels yet?" she asked.

"No. That's supposed to happen tomorrow, when he gets back." Carter turned back to Otto. "Did you bring everything?"

The big man nodded. "Six pounds of plastique and twelve detonators. Here."

Carter took the watertight belt and fastened it around his waist. "I'll plant the house and some of the outbuildings on my way back in."

"What time do we make them go boom?" Otto asked.

"Let's make it after dark. Seven should be good. They do love to eat and drink, and even with his troubles I don't think Bolivar will change his habits. They should be off their guard. By then I'll have my back up and will force Bolivar to let me start appraising the gems."

Carter stood, shook hands with Otto, and took Lorena by the elbow. He guided her outside the walls to the edge of the clearing and faced her.

"Now you have to make up your mind."

"I know," she said, averting her eyes.

"With or without the jewels, he'll run. Chances are he won't have much to run to. He wouldn't have expected all this to come down on him."

"What are you asking me?"

"You know damn well what I'm asking," Carter replied, putting a bite in his voice. "We both know the jewels are only half of this ball game. My half."

Her eyes came back to his, steady, unblinking. "I

don't know how I will do it, but I will do it. Bolivar is a dead man."

Carter nodded and called for Jorge to guide him back to the lake.

Revenge, he thought, is a very malignant disease.

It was slow going. Several of the guards had been pulled in off perimeter duty, so Carter had to evade for several minutes before he could climb the pipes and plant the last charge on the roof of the house.

The gray predawn light was just creeping into the sky when he lowered the spring ladder from the roof and dropped down into the hallway.

The house was quiet as he made his way to his bedroom.

He was just reaching for the knob, when it opened and Umberto Grossman stepped through the door. His fist was full of a very large magnum. A split second later the door behind him opened.

Carter whirled.

Bolivar, with a second magnum, confronted him.

"I've just had an interesting cable forwarded from one of my people in Rio."

"Oh?" Carter said, gauging his chances against the two revolvers.

"Yes, from Fabian Huzel. Just who the hell are you?"

Carter was about to reply, when a fist thudded into his kidneys. A sharp chop behind his right ear did the rest of the job.

All he saw was black as he hit the floor.

THIRTEEN

When Carter came to, his neck and right shoulder were a mass of pain, intense, throbbing pain. He lay on his belly, and perhaps another minute passed before he heard the groans. It was another minute before he realized they were his own.

Then he concentrated, first to stop making the silly noises, and then to find out where he was.

It wasn't easy.

He began with his fingers and then his toes. Everything moved. He opened his eyes. A window. Daylight. But his eyes wouldn't focus.

Fingers first, he pressed down, and groaned again as his shoulder muscles worked. Deliberately, he shut off the pain and continued to press until he sat up.

He looked around slowly, wary of what he might find.

And then he saw her. She sat in a chair at a table; the

single eye that wasn't swollen shut stared fixedly at him. One side of her face was a swollen, purple bruise. He could see fear crawling slowly, obscenely across the rest of her face.

"Who are you?" Her voice sounded as if someone had been beating a tattoo on her vocal cords.

"I need a drink. Water." She made no move. His hands slipped and he almost fell from the bed, then pushed himself up again.

Verna Rashkin stood and laboriously moved across the room to a sink. She filled a glass of water and staggered back until she stood in front of Carter.

"Who are you? They said you weren't Huzel."

"I'm a con man and a thief," he growled.

He reached for the water and she threw it in his face. Then she turned and made her way back to the chair. She barely made it, when the door opened and Umberto Grossman entered. A second man took up a post by the door.

"Who are you?"

"Christ," Carter hissed, "everybody around here has the narrowest vocabulary I've—"

The side of Grossman's foot caught him in the ribs, sending him reeling from the bed. When Grossman stepped forward for another kick, Carter was ready. He grabbed the foot and twisted. As Grossman fell, Carter used the leverage to gain his own footing.

But the room was spinning. He drew his foot back to stomp Grossman, but there the motor action ended.

The stormtrooper type at the door leaped forward and got an armlock around Carter's neck. He was held while Grossman scrambled to his feet and slammed Carter low in the gut.

The guard let go and Grossman hit Carter in the face, rocking him groggily against the wall. He hit Carter again, slamming his head against the wall. His legs turned to water and he slid slowly down the wall, trying to protect his face with his arms.

"We know what you did to Huzel. He escaped from your dungeon, or whatever it was. He is flying to Rio now. Who are you!"

"A thief . . . I'm a thief."

"You are a fool," Grossman grunted, and went to work with his feet.

Carter was slipping away, when from somewhere far off he heard a voice, Bolivar's, telling Grossman to stop, that he would be of no use to them dead . . . not yet.

The door slammed, and Carter did slip off for a few moments. Gradually, his mind began to activate again. He felt his head being raised and then life-giving water was flowing down his throat.

He opened his eyes and saw Verna's beaten face. "Thanks."

"You really must be a thief," she said, "or one hell of a fool."

"Grossman do that to you?"

She shook her head. "Eva. She loved it. I thought *I* was kinky. She's gone."

"Where are we?"

"In a room above the stable."

Somehow, with her help, Carter got to his feet and across the room to the sink. He turned the tap on full, cold, and put his head under. He came up for air and did it again.

It helped. When he wiped the water from his eyes,

they worked. Now he could take a hard look at Verna. The fear was still in her eyes, only now it looked as if she was on the border of hysteria.

"You look like hell."

She nodded. "I feel worse." She stepped forward and leaned against his chest. There were no tears. Verna wasn't the type for tears. But her body was shaking. "They're going to kill us, aren't they," she whispered.

"They're probably going to try," Carter said, and set her gently on the bed. "But I think there's time to do something about it."

And then it hit him. *Time*.

He looked at his wrist. His watch was smashed, stopped. "Verna, your watch . . . does it work?"

"Yeah . . . it's noon. Why?"

He remembered the bugs in his room. "Nothing. I have a thing about time, I hate to lose it."

He cased the room. The smell of leather made him guess that it had once been a tack room. The window wasn't barred, but there was heavy mesh over it and there were four panes in it. He'd have to kick the glass and the metal ribbing out before he could even get to the mesh.

In the stableyard below he could see a guard lounging against the wall. He had an M-16 slung over his shoulder, and his eyes were looking right at Carter in the window.

The door was solid wood, inches thick. He tried it, very gently, knowing it would be locked. He stood against the door, ear under the sharply angled ventilating slats, and listened. Someone moved, and paused for a long time, and moved again, this time with a slight *click-click* that Carter knew to come from a gun swivel. A guard.

He looked around some more. He needed a weapon, a club, anything. Seven hours until boom-boom time. He had to be off and running before then.

Then the bed came to mind. He lifted the springs and found a hardwood slat. It was broad for his hand, but solid and heavy.

Verna was watching him. "Against . . ."

He put a finger over her lips and then his lips at her ear. "To use an old cliché, the walls have ears."

For some reason that brought life. "Bastards!" she yelled. "You're all bastards!"

He couldn't use the slat until seven. He replaced it and stretched out on the bed. "There's nothing we can do. We might as well rest."

"You're right," she sighed, and stretched out beside him. She was silent for several moments, then, "You know, I still don't like you."

"I affect some people that way," Carter said with a yawn.

It was a little after four. Verna was asleep on the bed. Carter was at the window. He had been there for some time. It allowed him a good view of the helicopter.

For the past half hour, men had been shuttling from the house to the chopper and back. They had carried file boxes and briefcases, and now and then an occasional suitcase.

Bolivar was running, but not for good. If he were leaving with no intent of coming back, the Killmaster was fairly sure the man's greed would dictate evacuating the works of art scattered around the house.

So far, everything that had been taken to the chopper seemed to relate to business. More than likely he had found a safe place to settle in until the heat on him would blow over and he could quietly return and liquidate before finding a new hole to crawl into.

Where were the jewels? On the chopper? Perhaps. Or maybe not on the estate at all. Maybe they had been in Rio, in a safe-deposit box, all along.

There was a sound at the door and Carter moved away from the window, on his feet, ready. The door swung open and Umberto Grossman stood in its frame, an automatic like a toy in his big fist. He looked at the sleeping woman, then at Carter, and rolled his head toward the outside.

"He wants to see you."

They moved in procession, a guard in front, Carter and Grossman, and a second guard bringing up the rear.

"I would like to kill you very slowly," Grossman muttered out of the side of his mouth.

"You've already had a good start," Carter said dryly.

Grossman ignored him. "Bolivar wants to make a deal with you. I would advise you to take it."

They crossed the compound and entered the big house. Carter noticed that several guards were strung along the way.

Good, he thought; the perimeter of the estate would probably be like a sieve.

They entered the great room, where Bolivar sat at the end of the long dining table. In front of him and on the floor by his side were open file boxes. With glasses on the edge of his nose, Bolivar was refiling some papers and discarding others into the roaring fire behind him.

There was a second chair to his left. Carter felt the

hairs ripple on the back of his neck. On the table in front of that chair were two large leather cases. They were flat and rectangular.

"Sit," Bolivar said without looking up.

Carter sat. "Can I have a cigarette?"

Bolivar nodded. Grossman shoved one between Carter's lips and lit it, not worrying much if the flame caught Carter's nose as well.

The old man finished with his current pile of papers and looked up, removing his glasses.

"I managed to get through by telephone to Huzel in Amsterdam. He told me everything that he couldn't put in a cable."

Carter crushed out the cigarette, resisting the urge to ask how Huzel had escaped from Mortimer Potts. He also hoped that Potts was alive.

"Why did you take Huzel's place?" Bolivar continued.

Carter leaned back calmly. "I have fair contacts. I got the word you were selling. I wanted to make a good score. I took Huzel out and impersonated him."

Bolivar grimaced. "I wish I could believe that."

Carter shrugged. "It's true."

"I have done extensive research over the years. Very few dealers are financially able to convert a buy of this size. If you were one of them, I would know about you. Who are you?"

Carter shook his head. "I can get the cash. You have the merchandise. Once we made a deal, I didn't want to look over my shoulder while I was converting it."

This seemed to make Bolivar pause to think. It was a full two minutes before he glanced over Carter's shoulder and nodded. Grossman stepped forward and opened the two leather cases.

Suddenly the room seemed to explode with new light and color, all of it emanating from the interior of the cases.

Random unset jewels—diamonds, emeralds, and rubies—gleamed from their personalized niches in the layers of felt. The display was dazzling, and in the center of one case was the most dazzling of all... the bloodred, huge Heartstone.

"As you can see, I did not bring people here for nothing," Bolivar grunted. "Now I would like to know your source of finances."

"I can give you a number and a code," Carter lied. "A lot of my financing is through certain gentlemens' accounts in Switzerland, of course."

"Of course," Bolivar replied dryly. "How much of it is through Odessa?"

Carter looked as perplexed as possible. "What?"

"Odessa, you son of a bitch," Bolivar hissed. "Were you supposed to lure me somewhere else to settle the deal, or were you going to try and assassinate me right here?" He was on his feet now, his eyes full of fury and his face flushed.

"Odessa is a bunch of dying old men," Carter retorted, standing himself. "I don't know what the hell—"

Behind Carter, Grossman tried to kidney-punch him. The Killmaster slid to the side, avoiding the punch, and whirled. He brought his knee up into Grossman's crotch with enough force to drive the man's sex up into his belly. Grossman doubled with pain and fell to the floor.

It was futile and Carter knew it. Both guards rushed him from the rear of the room. They covered him like an avalanche and he went down under their combined weight.

Bolivar leaned over him, his florid face only inches above Carter's. "You're going to die. But before you do, you're going to let your contact know that your mission was completed. It won't free me forever, but it will buy me time. Take him back to the stables!"

They half dragged, half carried him back across the compound and up the steps. He was thrown into the room with such force that he bounced off the opposite wall beside the window.

Verna was awake, sitting wide-eyed on the bed staring at him. Carter motioned her to him with a wagging finger. She moved like a zombie and crouched beside him. He twisted her wrist around and looked at her watch.

It was almost six o'clock.

FOURTEEN

The time was near. He might even be cutting it too close. He glanced at Verna. Thankfully, some of the fear in her eyes had been replaced by a resolute anger.

Out the window he could see that her plea to the guard had worked. The Amazon, Eva, was hurrying across the courtyard.

He had gone over the entire room and found it bug-free. Their biggest hope now was twofold. One, that Eva would be very sure of her position and enter the room alone. Two, that what Carter had to say would sap her caution long enough.

Verna sat on the bed. Carter stood by the window in full view of the slot in the door. The smooth shard of windowpane that he had removed from the cracked window was on the window ledge behind him, carefully wrapped in his handkerchief. The hardwood slat was between the mattress and the box springs, easily available.

They heard the thud of the guard's boots and the click of Eva's heels on the stairs.

Carter glanced at Verna. "Can you do it?"

"I can do it," she replied, tight-lipped.

The footsteps stopped at the door. Carter couldn't see the guard's eye at the slit, but he knew it was there.

The door opened. The guard stepped in, his rifle ready. Eva moved right in behind him, a revolver held loosely in her right hand. The guard covered Carter with the rifle. Eva turned to Verna.

"Well, what is it you think you have to tell me that is so important?"

"It isn't her," Carter said quietly, "it's me."

She whirled. "You?"

"That's right."

"Well, speak!"

Carter shook his head. "In private."

Eva glanced at the guard and hooded her eyes in thought. The Killmaster was gambling that she would accept the idea that he thought he might get a better deal from her than he would from Bolivar.

He reinforced it. "I had a last word from Bolivar. Evidently he doesn't care about knowing the whole story any longer. I thought you might."

He could see the wheels turning in her blond head. She would run to Bolivar with anything he told her, but perhaps she could convince Carter that she would intercede for his life.

She made up her mind and turned to the guard. "Outside. I'll call you if I need you."

Reluctantly, the guard backed from the room. The door closed but the lock didn't click.

Eva turned to face Carter. "Well?"

"In private," he said.

She glanced at Verna. The woman was doing a good job. She was on the bed, slumped back against the wall, her eyes vacant and staring. The big woman decided to take her chances and advanced on Carter, stopping a few feet from him.

"What is it?" she murmured.

"Bolivar was only half right," Carter said in a voice barely above a whisper.

"Half right?" Eva replied, matching his volume.

"He accused me of coming here to kill him. It's true, that's what I was hired to do."

"So, and who hired you to do this?"

"I want your word that you'll get me out of here. I don't care about her, you can do what you want with her."

Carter had kept lowering his voice. To hear better, Eva had inched forward as he talked. The revolver was still pointed in his direction, but in her curiosity it was still being held with a loose hand.

"Names . . . tell me the names," she hissed.

"No names. I don't know them. A contact and the organization."

The woman smiled. "It is Odessa."

"No."

"Then who?"

Verna had the slat free from between the mattress and box springs. It was held in two steady hands over her shoulder as she advanced. Carter kept his eyes steady on Eva's.

. "Take me into the jungle, a head start of two miles. Just you and your gun. Then I'll tell you."

Her eyes narrowed. "How do you know I just won't kill you in the jungle after you tell me?"

Carter smiled. "I don't. But it's a better chance than I've got here, don't you agree?"

"Yes, that's true. I—"

The blow coming partially across the back of the skull and the shoulder wasn't as clean as Carter would have liked, but it did the job. Eva grunted in pain and shock and fell forward.

Carter chopped her wrist with his left hand, sending the revolver slithering across the room. He grabbed the handkerchief-wrapped glass with his right.

The woman had a lot of strength and fortitude. She was about to scream, when Carter grabbed the long braid of blond hair that hung down her back. In one smooth motion he jerked the braid tight around her throat so she couldn't scream. He looped it cruelly into the softness of her flesh and drove her to the floor by pressing his knee into her belly.

Wide with shock, her eyes stared up into his as he flashed the shard of glass in front of her face.

"No sound," he hissed. "Blink if you understand."

She remained motionless, either from fear or defiance. He moved the razorlike sliver back and forth in front of her eyes and leaned forward to whisper.

"One sound and I'll gouge out your eyes. One kick or squeal and I'll leave two raw holes in your face. Well?"

White and contorted, her face twitched and finally her eyes blinked several times. He eased off the twisted braid of hair just enough to give her air.

"I'm going to lift you up, Eva, and walk you to the door."

Her breath made a hissing sound and terror was in her eyes. Carter took his knee from her body and tugged on the braid, lifting. She swayed on her feet. He led her to the door, changed grips on the hair so that he stood to one side and partly behind her. He showed her the sharp spear of glass again.

"Verna, get the gun. Now unload it. Good, now hand it to her."

"I'd like to pistol-whip her with it," Verna spat.

"I'm sure you would, but this is more important."

"You'll never get as far as the jungle," Eva cracked. "There are no roads, there—"

"Shut up," Carter growled. "Verna, give her the gun."

Verna placed the revolver in the larger woman's hands and stepped to the center of the room.

"Okay, what's the guard's name outside the door?"

"Donner," Eva replied.

"It'd better be. Call out, tell him to come in here. If his name isn't Donner and he gets edgy, I'll slit your throat."

He maneuvered the big woman so that, through the slit, the guard could see Eva, still holding the gun, and most of Verna's body.

"All right . . . *now*!" Carter spat.

"Donner . . . Donner, come in, I am finished."

Footsteps. A pause while the man, more from force of habit than anything else, peered through the slit. Then the door opened and he walked into the room.

Behind Eva's back, Carter had already dropped the shard of glass and picked up the hardwood slat.

In one movement, he jerked Eva to her knees and swung the slat with all his strength.

The blow drove the man down and forward. His gun slid across the floor. Still hanging on to Eva's braid, Carter heeled the man in the throat. The guard gasped on the floor, his legs twitching. Carter dragged Eva to the gun, picked it up, and wheeled to drive its butt savagely into the bridge of the guard's nose. Grunting softly, he struck twice more. The sounds were wet and crunching.

He hauled the big woman across the man's body to close the door, lightening his grip to let her gasp a breath as he made sure the guard was dead. He was about to turn, when he heard a sickening crunch. He looked around.

Verna had retrieved the empty revolver when Eva had dropped it. She had reversed it and split the big blonde's skull with the butt. She was about to land a second blow, when Carter spoke.

"No need for that."

"Oh, yes, there is."

Carter took the gun from her hand. "No. In about five minutes this building is going sky-high. She'll go with it."

He got the shells from the bed and reloaded the revolver, then stuck it in his belt. He flipped off the safety and handed Verna the rifle.

"Can you use this?"

"I can point it and pull the trigger."

"Good. Just don't point it at me, and don't pull the trigger until I tell you to." Carter grabbed the blanket off the bed. "Let's go!"

They moved quietly down the narrow passageway

and then down the stairs. There was a guard lounging against one jamb of the open stable doors. His rifle was slung carelessly over one shoulder.

Carter was on top of him before the man knew he was there. Carter flipped the blanket over his head and then curled it tightly.

While the guard was trying to tear off the blanket, Carter hit him three times with everything he had. His fist sank each time wrist-deep into his gut, and the guard folded like a jackknife. Carter stood over him while he crouched on his knees with his hands clamped to his belly. He sucked breath into his tortured lungs and sobbed with pain.

Carter had all the time in the world to measure carefully and swing.

His knuckles hit him with such fury he hurtled backward horizontally, his nostrils dissolving into red as his shoulders thumped the ground.

He lay blowing red bubbles and Carter strode across to him, dragged him to his feet, shook him until he pawed the air in a weak show of defense, and then battered him to the ground again.

Carter gave no quarter. His knuckles were bone hammers. Every time the man fell, Carter dragged him to his feet and beat him into insensibility while he stood. The Killmaster battered his chest, ribs and abdomen, and pounded his face until his piggy eyes could no longer see and his mouth and nostrils were a red maw of bleeding flesh.

Then Carter stepped back and let him fall.

"My God," Verna gasped at his elbow.

"It was the quiet way," Carter said, lifting the man's legs and tugging him deeper into the stables.

"What now?"

"You see the barn over there with the flat roof across the top?" he asked, checking the second guard's rifle and slinging it.

"I see it."

"We're going over there. You're going up on that flat part of the roof. Then you're going to lie down and point your rifle at the house."

"Damn."

"What's wrong?"

"I'm afraid of heights."

"You'll just have to get over it. This way. There's another guard in the courtyard between here and this building."

"Wait a minute," she whispered, grabbing his arm.

"What?"

"You said you attached explosives to all these buildings."

"Not that one," he replied. "That's where the horses are. I'm an animal lover. C'mon, and stay in the shadows!"

At the last second he grabbed the dead guard's wide-brimmed hat and jammed it on his head.

He led the way for fifty feet, a hundred, a hundred and fifty, and then he stopped, straining his ears and trying to pick up any alien sound.

When he heard nothing, he grabbed Verna's hand and pulled her into the stables.

"That's the ladder to the hayloft. When you get up there you'll find another ladder that leads through the hole in the roof, there. See it?"

"I see it," she said grimly, and started up the ladder.

"And remember," Carter added, "shoot just for the

house. We've got help coming out of the jungle."

He waited until he saw her figure move through the hole in the roof, and then he moved back outside.

He was skirting the trees on the edge of the other outbuildings when the first explosion went off.

FIFTEEN

Carter was about to bolt for the courtyard between the old, unused stables and the house, when the stables went up. It wasn't a huge explosion, but it was quickly followed by fire that lit up the whole area.

The guard who had been in the courtyard careened around the corner.

Carter fired twice at the middle of the big, bulky body with the revolver. It kicked solidly against the heel of his palm and the man took two more steps toward him.

He was bent slightly at the waist and raising his gun as he advanced. His breath was very loud, but he seemed to be smiling; his lips were drawn back flat, exposing his teeth, and his face was wrinkled like a wadded-up piece of wastepaper.

Carter fired again and the man twisted sideways, bending sharply now, and his gun exploded into the

ground. He fell limply, disjointedly, like a big sack of
rags rolling onto its side. There was no longer the illu-
sion of a smile on his face; he looked surprised and
slightly stupid. That was all.

One wing of the house went up, and then the rest of
the perimeter's buildings also exploded.

It was like daylight now, and Carter could hear firing
coming from the jungle. That would be Lorena and Otto
wading their way through the perimeter guards.

Suddenly a female scream pierced the chaos of sound
around him, and Carter looked up. The old stable master was wrenching the rifle away from Verna. The
scream was her slipping from the edge of the roof.

Carter unslung the rifle and got off two fast rounds.
The old man grabbed his middle and disappeared
through the hole in the roof.

Carter ran around the building and spotted Verna at
once. She lay on her back, her arms and legs sprawled
like those of a broken doll. He knew she was dead even
before he saw the staring look of her eyes. She wasn't
pretty anymore, she wasn't anything. The exquisitely
sculptured head was like the relief on an old Roman
coin: distant, cold, remote.

He turned and headed for the main house.

Halfway there, a guard ran from one of the rear
doors. He was holding his hands up, palms out. "Don't
go in, don't go in!" he shouted.

Carter shot him and leaped over the body. He ran
around the wide veranda until he reached the part of the
house that was not in flames. He was about to kick open
one of the doors, when Otto von Krumm and one of
Buck Waters's locals rounded the corner in front of him.

Otto didn't mince words. "How many did you get so far?"

"Four," Carter replied.

"We got three coming out the side, and one was crunched jumping from a third-floor window," Otto grunted.

"That should leave three, besides Bolivar and Grossman. What about the servants?"

"They scattered. I don't know if they all made it. We let them through."

"Where's Lorena?" Carter barked.

Otto paused for only an instant. "She went in the front, just shooting her way inside. I couldn't stop her."

"I didn't figure you could. Stay out here, make sure no one gets through."

Without waiting for a reply, Carter kicked the door open and burst through it into the smoky interior. He found himself in the enormous kitchen.

Half by sight, half by feel, he found a hand towel and soaked it under the tap. When it was wrapped securely around his face, he hit the small dining room and went on into a sitting room.

The deeper he went, the greater was the smoke. As yet, he had seen no flames on the inside, but they would be in the bedroom areas on the upper story.

He had to kick the door of the great room several times before he could get it open. When he did, he saw the body that had been sprawled against it.

The files and papers that had been spread on the long table were now scattered across the floor. He saw no sign of the two leather cases.

Halfway up the stairs he saw another guard sprawled.

He was cut almost in half, with his rifle still slung over his shoulder.

There wasn't a sound now except the crackling of flames on the floors above Carter.

Suddenly there was a single shot. It was quickly followed by a staccato burst from an automatic rifle.

Carter took the stairs two at a time. Halfway up, the last guard appeared at the top of the stairs.

Carter raised the rifle, but before he could fire, the man toppled forward. The Killmaster stepped aside and the body rolled past him, trailing a path of blood down the stairs.

Carter leaped to the landing and shouted: "Lorena . . . Lorena, where are you!"

A door opened behind him and he dived for the floor. He rolled up against the wood-paneled wall as the hall filled with the staccato roar of a submachine gun. The wood a foot from his face chipped away as though a buzz saw were chewing it.

He rolled away to avoid the splinters and return the fire. Two shots from the automatic rifle and it clicked empty.

Carter cursed and pawed for the revolver in his belt. It was gone, lost when he had hit the floor.

The shooter had heard, too, and was now running toward him. Carter rolled in the smoke, avoiding the bullets.

The man lost Carter in the smoky darkness just long enough for the Killmaster to reach up and grab him. He got the gun arm with one hand, spun around, and brought it over his shoulder. He got the other hand on his wrist and yanked. The man had to either come up or risk a broken elbow.

He took the risk.

Carter heard the bone crack and the machine pistol clattered down the stairs.

The man hit the floor and came right back up to his feet.

The smoke cleared just enough then for Carter to see.

It was Umberto Grossman.

"Good!" he roared. "Before this place falls in on us, I will have the joy of killing you!"

Grossman was fast, like lightning, and deadly, even with one broken arm and his lungs full of smoke.

He came in from Carter's right, went from high to low, and suddenly appeared on the Killmaster's left, his own good side. A swift, blurring chop came at Carter's neck from the man's healthy right arm.

Carter blocked it, but caught a kick in his left side that sent him reeling. He bounced off the wall and started to turn. Something chopped him across the neck. Carter spun, reaching.

The room turned end over end. He landed hard on his shoulders, breath gusting out in a rush. A shoe heel drove viciously at his throat, and he was barely alert enough to roll dizzily away from it. The second try caught him on the side of the jaw. Red lights flashed on and off, on and off.

Grunting, the Killmaster pawed at the floor and came up, shaking his head, trying to push the red spots out of his eyes. The knife edge of a calloused palm lanced into his throat. He swayed on his knees, sucking through the bright, hard agony that wouldn't let the air pass. The face floating over him was out of focus, hazy, leering at him, full of pure evil.

Carter wobbled up and stuck a fist at it, felt the hand

snap around his wrist, felt himself yanked off-balance and knew something painful was on its way. But the hand slipped off. The face moved back, jerked back. Carter spat, pumped a gulp of head-clearing air into his chest.

Grossman was on his knees, reaching up with his one good arm to get a madwoman off his back.

Lorena was riding him, her legs around his middle. One hand clenched his hair, the claws of her other hand dug into his eyes. Her fingers already dripped with blood as she ripped frantically at his face.

Grossman screamed in pain and tried to unseat her.

Chin pulled in, gasping, Carter moved forward as the mist in front of his own eyes cleared. "Lorena!" he cried. "Let him go, I've got him!"

He got his fingers twisted into the man's jacket. Screaming in pain, Grossman struck out with his good hand and arm, but it was useless with his blinded eyes.

Lorena dropped away.

Carter pulled him off the floor, held him in midair, and wrapped his other hand around the man's ankle. Then he turned slowly and hammered Grossman's head against the wall. Plaster cracked. Dust geysered. Carter swung him back for another stroke, and another, shaking and ruining the wall. Finally Grossman stopped screaming. Carter dropped him into the dusty pile of plaster.

The Killmaster didn't need to check. Umberto Grossman was dead. He found the revolver and waddled his way through the smoke.

"Lorena . . . ?" he shouted, stumbling down the hall. "Lorena!"

He had planted the explosive on the roof. It was

gone, or at least most of it, and the flames were eating their way downward. If there had been a high wind, the house would have already been devoured. As it was, on such a calm night and with the lack of wind, it was moving slowly.

Slowly, Carter thought as he slammed door after door open, *but surely.*

"Lorena!"

Still no answer.

Suddenly he burst through the last door in the wing and found them.

It was a sight out of hell.

Bolivar was on a satin-covered settee. He sat, slightly hunched over, his hands clasped over his middle. Blood oozed in waves through his fingers. His eyes were bright, alert. He even looked up as Carter entered the room.

A few feet in front of him, Lorena was on her knees, much in the same position as Bolivar, her hands clasped over her middle.

Carter was frozen in time and space.

They were talking, actually seemed to be chatting.

Between them on the floor, scattered like so many pieces of pretty glass, was a fortune in gemstones.

Slowly, through the shock and the smoke filling his mind and the room, Carter heard the conversation.

"Your brother," Bolivar was saying, "is an evil man. You were a child, a baby. To raise you with revenge all these years was a waste."

"No," Lorena replied calmly, "every minute was worth it . . . for this."

Carter could believe neither his eyes nor his ears.

"And what have you gained?" Bolivar gasped, his

life pumping out from between his fingers. "Your family baubles back?"

"No . . . no, no, no," Lorena whispered. "I've gained more, much more. I've been able to shoot you in the belly and watch you die, very slowly."

Bolivar shook his head, coughed blood, and looked up at Carter. "Who are you . . . Odessa?"

"Does it matter?" Carter replied, amazed at himself with the flames creeping around them all that he could be so calm.

"He's just a man," Lorena said, "a hired hand, a conduit to get me to you."

For the first time since Carter had met him, Bolivar laughed out loud. Blood poured from his mouth and there was a hacking sound, but still he laughed.

And then suddenly he stopped.

He removed one hand from his punctured belly and waved it at the floor.

"Then take your payment, man. Gather them up!" He laughed some more.

Carter ignored him. He turned to Lorena and tried to lift her to her feet. "We've got to get out of here."

"No!" she cried.

"Yes!" Carter screamed at her, fighting the fury of her resistance.

"No! I want to watch him die!"

"Don't be a fool," Carter hissed. "He's a dead man. You've got the revenge you came for."

"No. Not yet."

"Yes!" Carter cried, yanking her to her feet. "He's an old man. He's dying and he knows it and he doesn't care."

Another laugh from the near-dead man on the settee.

"We're all dead, or waiting to die. What's the difference? Leave her. But take the jewels. They'll only be found by ignorant Indians."

Carter's mind was glazing over, like his eyes. He found it impossible to breathe.

Lorena had wrenched herself from his grasp. She was on her hands and knees on the floor. He stumbled toward her, but she managed to elude his grasp.

"There!" she cried, suddenly coming back to her feet with her hands cupped beneath his chin. "Look!"

Carter looked down. In her cupped hands were several diamonds, glittering even in the thickening smoke.

And in their center was the enormous symbol of a lost world, a dead monarchy.

The Heartstone.

"We have it!" she said.

"Yeah," Carter replied, seeing the madness in her eyes that he had always known was there but had never admitted. "Now, we go."

She shoved the stones into Carter's pocket and turned back to face Bolivar. "He's still dying."

Carter pulled the revolver from his belt, aimed, and put a slug right between Bolivar's eyes.

"Not now he isn't."

He slung Lorena over his shoulder and ran out into the hall and down the stairs.

SIXTEEN

Carter stood at the window. Outside, he watched the Amsterdam street come alive with whores, pickpockets, hippies, and good, honest foreign businessmen out to get laid.

"He was a good man."

Carter turned. The beautiful Oriental girl sat at the desk, her brother standing beside her, his hand on her shoulder.

"I wouldn't think about it if I were you," Carter said. "Mortimer always had a will, even when he didn't have anything to leave anyone."

"It was nice service, yes?" the girl said.

"Yes, a very nice service," Carter replied, forcing his face to remain stone.

Otto had got them out by boat, down the long river. Then there had been a charter to the Canary Islands and a commercial jet to Frankfurt.

At the castle they had found Mortimer Potts with his neck broken, crucified to some timbers in the basement.

Fabian Huzel didn't just kill. He took gleeful delight in the killing.

Otto knew a doctor. The cause of death was listed as a heart attack. Mortimer had been cremated and his ashes brought back to the Yum-Yum Club.

"We were so poor," the girl said, "and now we are so rich."

"Don't worry about it," Carter said. "If Mortimer hadn't wanted you to have everything, he wouldn't have given you everything in his will. Live, enjoy . . . that's what Mortimer did."

Carter headed for the door.

"Mr. Carter," the girl said, "if there is ever anything . . ."

Carter smiled. "There might be . . . and if you did it, you'd just be carrying on Mortimer's tradition."

He left the Yum-Yum Club. A block away he crawled into the front seat of a black Mercedes. Otto was behind the wheel.

"How did you do?" Carter asked.

"Very well, actually," came the stoic reply. "A little over a million and a half, American, for the diamonds. The two emeralds brought forty thousand per."

"That should take care of you . . . and her," Carter said.

Otto smiled. "Leave it to me, Nick. I'll have her back on her feet in a year."

It was the way he said it that made Carter smile. "Otto, if I didn't know better, I'd say you were in love."

"Well," Otto shrugged, "it is about time for me to act my age. Shall we get on with it?"

"Yes," Carter nodded, "let's. You're sure everything the baroness has is traceable?"

"Oh, God, yes."

It was early morning, the dead hour, the hour of the ultimate thief.

The Mercedes barely paused as the darkly clad figure rolled from the door. In seconds he was over the fence.

The whole operation took less than seven minutes. Break in, go up to the attic—past the master bedroom, the nursery, the empty guest room, the maid's room where the au pair girl dreamed of warmth and sunshine and lemon trees—up to the deserted attic, a little of toys, books, discarded furniture, the squeak of a rusty window hinge, and Carter was on the roof, moving velvet-pawed across the leaded guttering to the attic window in the house.

He used a diamond with four neat strokes, waited for the glass to fall—a tiny brittle whisper of noise—then put his hand into the hole he had made, opened the window, and lowered himself into the house.

In the comfortable darkness he moved through the house. The stairs were carpeted and the noise he made was less than a sigh; he went down to the drawing room.

He already knew the location of the safe. Finding it in the darkness took two minutes, opening it another five.

The Baroness Erica von Steinholtz wouldn't realize for a full twenty-four hours that two million dollars' worth of her family's fabulous fortune in jewels was gone.

•　•　•

Nadia Grinzel had a chubby face. It was the sort of face one sees on Scandinavian dolls in shop windows at Christmastime: cream and pink porcelain with sculptured lips and eyebrows, a pointed little nose, ears, barely visible at the lobes, that peeked out beneath yellow, spun-candy hair that fitted on top of her head like an elegant bathing cap. Her eyes were magnified by a large pair of heavy-rimmed, tortoiseshell glasses that usually hung from a gold chain looped around the back of her neck.

Nadia Grinzel's I.Q. matched her vision: 40-40.

When the phone rang that night, she was dressing for an evening out. The reason for the evening out was a young banker, rich, handsome, and almost as dumb as Nadia.

She fully expected him to ask for her hand.

That would be nice.

She had worked for Fabian Huzel for two years. It was better than being a whore in the Damrak—which she had briefly been—but not as good as trapping a banker. The phone rang.

"Yes?"

"Fräulein Grinzel?"

"Yes."

"This is Horst. I have the merchandise."

"Oh, God, not tonight."

"Yes, tonight."

"But I'm . . ."

"Fräulein Grinzel, this is business. I have just obtained the merchandise. Needless to say, I can't wait forever to get a price."

"Damn," she muttered under her breath, and then sighed. "All right. How long before you can get here?"

"I am on the corner, two minutes."

"Fine."

She killed the connection and dialed. When the old crone who always answered came on, Nadia was brief and to the point.

"I have a very large one. I must have a figure by noon tomorrow."

"*Ja*, very well. I will tell him."

Though it was not yet nine in the morning, a raw and rainy day looked in the windows of the old police central building overlooking the river.

A green-shaded lamp was burning above the desk of Chief Inspector Otis Konig Sev of the Metropolitan Amsterdam Police. He had been in his office since seven that morning, when the package had arrived. It contained papers that solved practically every major jewel robbery in the country for the past ten years.

Konig Sev examined the last of it, leaned back at ease, and smoked a cigarette with an air of doing so cynically. He was a long, stringy man whose thick and wrinkled eyelids gave him a sardonic look that was thoroughly deserved. Though he was not bald, his white hair had begun to recede from the skull as though in sympathy with the close cropping of his gray mustache. His eyes were bright, and right now they were amused.

The phone call had awakened him just before dawn that morning.

"Inspector Konig Sev?"

"Yes, yes, who is this?"

"Never mind. I understand you are very close to retirement, Herr Inspector."

"I don't enjoy being awakened from a sound sleep to be told what I already know."

A low chuckle from the other end of the line. "Early this morning, a package will be delivered to your office by courier. The package will contain records of the buying and selling of vast amounts of stolen gems."

"Damn you say." Konig Sev was upright in his bed now, alert.

"The records alone are only circumstantial. They alone probably won't convict the man. I'll give you something else that will."

Konig Sev was a cynical and rational man. "This is beginning to sound like a joke."

"No joke, Inspector, I assure you. Just before dawn yesterday morning, the house of Baron and Baroness von Steinholtz was burgled. All of the family jewels were stolen."

"My God, man, if such a robbery had occurred, it would have been reported!"

"Not really. The baron has been out of the city on business. The baroness has been confined to her bed with a cold."

Konig Sev was incredulous. "You mean . . . ?"

"Exactly, Inspector. Baroness von Steinholtz doesn't even know she's been robbed. I suggest you check it. I will call you later this morning in your office."

The caller had hung up and Konig Sev had rushed into his clothes. A call to his office had brought a car with two patrol officers to his house in minutes.

He couldn't suppress a laugh when he remembered the look on the face of Baroness von Steinholtz, and her comment, "Brilliant! Absolutely brilliant police work!"

The phone on his desk buzzed. "Yes?"

It was the central operator. "I think this is the call you've been waiting for, Inspector."

"Put him through." There was a series of clicks and he spoke again. "This is Inspector Konig Sev."

"I trust you've had an enlightening morning, Inspector?"

"Dammit, man, this is serious business. What do you know about the von Steinholtz robbery?"

"A great deal, but, more importantly, I know where the jewels will be between nine o'clock and noon today."

"I'm listening."

"Number Twelve Herengracht. The flat is Four-A. It is owned by a young lady named Nadia Grinzel. But she is only a drop. The man you want is Fabian Huzel."

"Huzel," Konig Sev whispered.

"Yes, Inspector. You can retire with honors."

The phone went dead, but Konig Sev kept holding it to his ear, staring off into space.

"Fabian Huzel," he muttered, "at last."

Nadia Grinzel checked through the peephole and unlocked the door. Fabian Huzel entered the flat shaking the water from his head and shoulders like a shaggy dog.

"Terrible day," he mumbled.

It was a comparatively small flat, one main room with a bedroom alcove, an open kitchen area, and a door to a bathroom. It was in a corner of the building, so there were windows on two sides.

Nadia had obviously been preparing breakfast. There was a table near the window, half set, and there were cooking sounds coming from the kitchen.

"Do you want coffee?"

"No, I don't have time. Where are they?"

"I'll get them," Nadia said. "I have to turn my stove down."

She fiddled with the stove and then stepped up on a low, three-step ladder. She moved aside a square section of the false ceiling and raised to her toes as she felt along the indentation of the neighboring section.

Behind her, Huzel shook his head. If the police ever searched the place, he thought, that would be the first place they would look.

Nadia stepped from the ladder and brought two heavy chamois bags to the table where Huzel sat.

"It's funny," he said as he untied the drawstring on the first bag. "I thought Horst Eberson was in prison in France."

The girl shrugged and sipped her coffee. "I've never had him before, but his name was on the list you gave me."

Huzel's eyes grew wide and saliva gathered at the corners of his mouth as he emptied the contents of the first bag.

He was examining the third piece through the loop in his eye socket when it struck him.

"Idiot!" he cried. "That damn idiot!"

"What's the matter?" Nadia almost spilled her coffee.

"A first-year clerk in any watch shop would recognize—"

It was at that moment the door shattered from its hinges and the flat filled with uniforms.

The Differt, a traditional Amsterdam *broodjeswinkel*, or café, was located at 15 Herengracht. Through its spotlessly clean front windows there was an excellent view of number 12.

Otto von Krumm pushed his plate away with a sigh and patted his belly. "A fine meal."

Carter sipped his second cup of coffee and nodded. "Every new day should be started with a good meal."

Suddenly a fierce light shone in Otto von Krumm's eyes and his lips parted in a leering grin.

"My, oh my."

"Something?"

"The time for joy has come, my friend. Just take a quick glance over your left shoulder."

Casually Carter turned his head.

The woman was taken down the steps of number 12 first. Her face was white with fear, and even at such a distance the Killmaster could see her lips tremble. A uniformed police officer was on each side of her, and her wrists were manacled together in front of her body.

Seconds later Fabian Huzel appeared, also with an officer on each side of him. The second party moved a little more slowly than the first. This was because Huzel's ankles, as well as his wrists, were cuffed.

His clothes were torn and in disarray. Thunder as well as a large, purplish bruise was on his glowering face.

"Looks like our boy gave them a bit of a tussle," Otto smirked.

"It would appear so," Carter agreed. "Hope they got some good licks in before he gave up."

"I do think they did," Otto replied. "From the looks of his face I'd say he'll have a great deal of trouble chewing his food for quite some time."

"I'd say that."

"Pity."

They watched until the pair were placed in separate cars and were driven away. In only a few minutes the curious dispersed and the quiet neighborhood returned to normal.

The two then took their time finishing their coffee. Carter paid, leaving a large tip, and they walked the two blocks to the waiting Mercedes.

The Killmaster checked his watch as he slid into the passenger side seat.

"I should just make the one-ten flight to Vienna without too boring a wait."

Otto pulled from the curb into the light noonday traffic. He was whistling softly. "How long do you think he'll get?"

Carter frowned in concentration. "I'd say thirty years, give or take."

Otto laughed. "With the thieves he'll take with him I'll give you ten to one he won't last five years."

Carter leaned back in the seat with a broad smile on his face. "I don't take sucker bets, you know that, Otto."

SEVENTEEN

The plane landed at Vienna's airport just past four in the afternoon. Carter cabbed to the hotel and checked in with his own name and passport.

In his room he built a drink and moved to the window to stare out at the city.

The elation of nailing Fabian Huzel had passed by now. He didn't look forward to the coming evening, the meeting he had agreed to make, and the rehashing of the whole mess that would be expected of him.

He would rather forget it, catch a plane down to Nice, and lay on the beach for a week.

A week, hell, he thought—better a month.

But there was the list.

The goddamned list.

* * *

He had already code telexed his report back to Washington. He knew Hawk and the whole section would be elated.

Elated?

They were probably frothing at the mouth in anticipation. A lot of bodies would fall when he sent in the list. He wondered how many would be buried where they fell.

He napped for a couple of hours and then took a long shower. By the time he was dressed and on the street it was dark and a wind had come up.

Since it was only a few blocks and he was a bit early, he walked. The sky was clear. It would be cold and crisp tomorrow, but the sun would probably come out.

Café Josef was a small, quiet place with imitation black leather walls, comfortable furniture, and discreet lighting. It was about half full when Carter entered.

"One, sir?"

"I'm expecting a friend."

"Of course. This way."

Carter followed him to a front table that looked out on the boulevard. He ordered a scotch, neat, and sipped it as he waited.

He did not have to wait long. Hardly five minutes had passed when he saw her striding across the street with her determined walk. Gone were the corduroy slacks and the leather jacket. She wore a stylish raincoat that flapped open now and then to reveal a figure-fitting black skirt and a frilly white blouse.

If one didn't know better, he thought, one would suppose that she was an actual flesh-and-blood woman.

It was hard for Carter.

He remembered too well the blonde's face when the bullet had struck her in the back and the ease with which Ilse Beddick had guided the burial in the frozen earth.

Inside, she stood for a moment looking over the room. When she spotted Carter she headed directly for the table.

As she approached, Carter stood up. Then he remembered himself and sat down as the waiter approached to seat her. She ordered wine and shrugged out of her coat.

Silence.

It was as if neither of them knew how to start.

"Congratulations," Carter said at last, "on getting out."

"Vadim set it up beforehand," she replied. "It was done with very little effort. Have you heard?"

Carter nodded. "Washington informed me."

"He died very quietly, in his sleep."

"Wonderful," Carter said.

She either ignored or had not caught the sarcasm in his voice. "I wish I could have given him the details but . . ."

She shrugged, truly sad.

The waiter set a glass of wine in front of her and left.

"But don't worry. I have what you want right in here."

She patted a slim clutch bag and then took a cloisonné case from it and extracted a cigarette. As Carter flicked his lighter he didn't try to hide the wince on his face he felt from her words.

"Is something troubling you?"

"A little. It was very messy."

She leaned forward. "I want to hear about it, every word, every detail."

Carter winced again. He signaled the waiter for another drink. When it came he took a deep breath and began in a voice barely above a whisper.

He talked for nearly an hour with Ilse Beddick's face not once changing expression. When he finished she seemed in deep thought for several minutes.

"And Lorena?"

"She is in a clinic near Wilhelmshaven in Germany. Here is the address." He passed a note across the table which she folded and placed in her purse without even glancing at it.

"She is being taken care of?"

"Quite. A man named Otto von Krumm thinks that he may well be in love with her. He'll take care of her. Perhaps Otto is even more wealthy than she is even after her . . . windfall."

Ilse thought this over and nodded again. "Good. You said she went a little mad. How mad?"

Killing mad, crazy mad, revenge mad, he thought.

"In my opinion?" he asked.

"I have no one else to ask."

"In my opinion," Carter said, rubbing his temples hard, "I think she is quite insane and will stay that way." He didn't add that she had her brother's lust for revenge to thank for it.

"You carried out every bit of our half of the contract. Here is your half."

Carter opened the envelope and pulled out three neatly typed pages. It was complete: names, addresses, telephone numbers, even current occupations. He slipped it into his jacket pocket.

"Satisfactory?" she asked.

"Very," Carter replied.

She slipped her arms into the sleeves of her coat.

"Where will you go?"

The question seemed to surprise her. She gave it some thought before answering.

"Somewhere far . . . where no one will ever find me."

"And forget about all this."

"No. Never. I'll remember it well."

"Yeah, I thought you would," Carter replied. "So will I. By the way, here."

He dropped the bloodred Heartstone into her hand. She looked down at it vacantly and then back up at Carter.

"I think it's better that you have it than Lorena. That is, if she ever does get her sanity back."

Ilse Beddick smiled for the first time since she had entered the restaurant.

"My, my, a sentimental killer."

She dropped the gem carelessly into her bag and walked from the restaurant.

Carter stared through the window after her until she was lost from sight.

"Will there be anything else, sir?"

"Yeah. Another scotch. Make it a triple and keep them coming until I tell you to stop."

DON'T MISS THE NEXT NEW
NICK CARTER SPY THRILLER

ARCTIC ABDUCTION

Carter awoke feeling better than he had for a long time. Even after the ordeal of the plane ride, he felt thoroughly restored. The discomfort of the stabbing in Washington had left him. His problem right now was breakfast. He could have eaten a polar bear roasted over a spit.

He lit the stove again and this time read Schmidt's instructions. The mug that sat on top could be filled with small packages included in the fare. They were Schmidt's own gourmet meals, in miniature, all able to fit into the oversize mug and be cooked in their own plastic bags.

When his stomach was satisfied, Carter unzipped the tent and scooped snow away from the front. The two duffel bags were still there, some of their goodies as yet unexamined. Carter's weapons were still in the bags, including two deadly gas bombs that he taped to his inner thigh. He'd thought about taping them just inside his parka, but old habits die hard. They would be concealed where hundreds of searchers had not discovered them over the years.

Carter examined his clothes. He put on a skintight black outfit that would have done a second-story man proud. Over this he climbed into the uniform of the Inspector General's Major Anatoly Marchenko. And over all this, he donned the down parka and snowmobile pants.

So what was he to do hundreds of miles from nowhere? The only compensation he had was his own anonymity.

He went through Schmidt's goods again and came across a box he hadn't examined before. It was a miniature compass on top and a sextant on the bottom. Carter spread an empty duffel bag on the snow, spread out the topographical map Schmidt had provided, and using the sextant, plotted his exact position. According to the scale on the Silva compass, he was only five miles from the coastal town of Guba. He took a bearing on the town, cleaned up the camp, and started out for Guba using the awkward snowshoe gait he'd learned earlier.

Every five minutes he took a sighting with his compass. He was in a sea of white. The snow was coming down in a light powder. He could see nothing but the tracks he'd made.

It took almost six hours to make the five miles, but he finally came to the outskirts of town. The first thing he was aware of was the barking of dogs. They weren't barking at him. They were secured to a sleigh and had been left waiting while their master visited in a low-slung hut.

The town was no more than a village. It would be

Eskimo, probably Inuit this close to the Bering Sea. Even here they should have a garrison and some equipment.

He spotted it without difficulty. A lone guard was posted outside a hut that was about twenty feet square. The Killmaster took off his snowshoes and secured them in a sling on his back. The snow had been packed to a hard base in the town. In his multiple layers of clothing he tested Hugo's release and was satisfied.

First he needed a slow recon of the town without being seen. A circle of the whole town took only five minutes. The smell of wood burning brought back memories of friendlier campfires. The object of his recon was parked behind the military shack, an industrial strength snow machine with skis in front and oversize twin tractors in back. It was large enough to satisfy his needs, but it had a trailer attached that would take time to disconnect.

Carter thought his plan through before making his move. He was at the back of the shack. It had three small windows, but they were completely frozen over. God, what a way to live, he thought as he approached the guard, trying not to let his boots crunch in the fresh snow.

The guard's vision was impaired by the size of his parka. He was turning to challenge the noise of crunching snow, his Kalashnikov at the ready, when the stiletto blade entered his side and punctured his heart. He stood still for a moment, his chest cavity flooding, then his knees started to sag and he went down, Carter easing him into the white carpet.

The Killmaster reached for Pierre, tore him from skin that was turning blue in the process, and opened the barracks door.

Four men occupied the hut. Two were in bunks, totally immobile. One was at a stove pouring coffee into a mug.

A third sat at a table playing a solitary game of cards. All eyes shifted to him, eyes that held no suspicion, only curiosity. Carter twisted the halves of Pierre, tossed it into the cabin, and bolted the door from the outside.

One burst of an AK-47 tore at the door over his head as he flopped to his belly. But the action was fast and ended quickly. No one survived the small bomb if they weren't expecting it. This was one of the few times he felt regret for the men inside, but they were the local military, the only ones who could have stopped him.

He moved to the back of the shack and examined the snow machine. The keys were not in it. He checked the gas tank. It was full. Several fifty-gallon drums of fuel stood nearby, half covered with snow, and it took him a few minutes to wrestle them into the sled.

He brushed off the machine, then moved back to the shack. By this time several of the locals were starting to move toward the shack. He picked up the automatic rifle of the fallen guard and waved off the locals. They moved slowly, so he hurried them along with a string of 7.62mm slugs at their feet.

The Killmaster took a deep breath and entered the cabin. The key was in the most obvious place possible, hanging from a nail on the inside of the door. The four men were dead. The one at the table had tried to blast the door. He had two grenades in his webbing. Carter put them in a pocket, disabled the radio, and headed for the snowmobile.

The battery was new. The machine turned over slowly but caught within seconds. Carter made a slow circle of the town again to make sure his snowshoe tracks were covered. The natives stayed indoors. Two smaller machines stood side by side at the rear of the largest hut, obviously the local meeting place.

The machines were undoubtedly the most valuable items the locals had ever owned. Their livelihood probably depended on them. But Carter had to weigh the harm to these civilians against the lives of more than a hundred American kids. He pulled the pin on one of the grenades and blew both machines into piles of scrap.

Something he'd seen nagged at him, and he was reluctant to leave without checking it out. An antenna. One of the huts had a shortwave antenna.

The Killmaster stopped the oversize snowmobile outside the hut and entered with his Luger in his hand. A young couple cowered in one corner, covering their children with their bodies.

"I'm sorry," Carter said as he put two 9mm bullets through the radio.

As he pulled away, the dogs were barking furiously. They still had the dogs. If they used the dogs, they could report him to the authorities. He pulled the pin on the second grenade and was about to blow the dogs and the sleigh to another dimension, but his conscience deflected his aim at the last moment. He tossed the high explosive at the back of the sled, shredding the runners.

The snow was still falling, not heavily but enough to cover his tracks to some extent. He gunned the machine. It responded sluggishly with all the gasoline in back, and he backtracked to his own camp.

The tent was still there and all of his equipment. He packed quickly, filling the two duffel bags. He tossed them on the back of the machine and started on the bearing he'd charted for Kivak.

The snow was falling hard now but he didn't care. It was a cloak to hide him from his enemies. He pulled on a pair of snow goggles and blessed Schmidt again. He had warm clothing, transportation, food, and plenty of fuel. He had two hundred miles of barren tundra to cover but he was prepared for it. This was the best way to come at them. He'd be lucky to see a tree or another settlement as he headed southeast. He was making about ten miles an hour. He'd make Kivak the following night or the morning after that. They would be forewarned. It didn't matter. He could attack at any time. His people would be at Eielson Air Force Base. A carrier was probably as close as they could get one to the winter ice floes.

Maybe they would give the C-32s air cover from Eielson. He really didn't care. When the time came, he would radio in and they would come. He'd seen Hawk's face and General Farmer's. He'd seen the determination register on the countenance of the President and he knew. They'd get the kids home if they had to send an armada and start World War III.

But it was up to him now. And he was getting close.

—From ARCTIC ABDUCTION
A New Nick Carter Spy Thriller
From Jove in April 1990